JUST WILLIAM ON HOLIDAY

1. Just – William
2. More William
3. William Again
4. William – The Fourth
5. Still – William
6. William – The Conqueror
7. William – The Outlaw
8. William – In Trouble
9. William – The Good
10. William
11. William – The Bad
12. William's Happy Days
13. William's Crowded Hours
14. William – The Pirate
15. William – The Rebel
16. William – The Gangster
17. William – The Detective
18. Sweet William
19. William – The Showman
20. William – The Dictator
21. William and Air Raid Precautions
22. William and the Evacuees
23. William Does His Bit
24. William Carries On
25. William and the Brains Trust
26. Just William's Luck
27. William – The Bold
28. William and the Tramp
29. William and the Moon Rocket
30. William and the Space Animal
31. William's Television Show
32. William – The Explorer
33. William's Treasure Trove
34. William and the Witch
35. William and the Pop Singers
36. William and the Masked Ranger
37. William the Superman
38. William the Lawless

Just – William a facsimile of the first (1922) edition
Just William – As Seen on TV
More Just William – As Seen on TV
William at War
Just William at Christmas
Just – William Through the Ages
The Woman Behind William: a life of Richmal Crompton by Mary Cadogan
School is a Waste of Time!
by William Brown (and Richmal Crompton)

"SHE DIDN'T RESCUE ME FROM DROWNING," SAID WILLIAM. "I RESCUED HER. SHE STRUGGLED SOMETHING TERRIBLE."

RICHMAL CROMPTON

Just William on Holiday

Illustrated by Thomas Henry

MACMILLAN
CHILDREN'S BOOKS

First published in the United Kingdom 1996 by
Macmillan Children's Books
A division of Macmillan Publishers Limited
25 Eccleston Place London SW1W 9NF and Basingstoke

Associated companies around the world

ISBN 0 333 65401 3

3 5 7 9 8 6 4 2

Phototypeset by Intype London Ltd
Printed and bound by Mackays of Chatham PLC, Chatham, Kent

CONTENTS

An invitation from William

You can join the Outlaws Club!

You will receive

*** a special Outlaws wallet containing**

your own Outlaws badge

the Club Rules

and

a letter from William giving you the secret password

To join the Club send a letter with your name and address written in block capitals telling us you want to join the Outlaws, and a postal order for £2.50 to

The Outlaws Club
Children's Marketing Department
25 Eccleston Place
London SW1W 9NF

You must live in the United Kingdom or the Republic of Ireland in order to join.

CHAPTER ONE

A SPOT OF HEROISM

WILLIAM SAT alone in the railway carriage and watched telegraph poles, cows and trees fly past the window. He was mildly interested in the sight and amused himself by pretending that it was the train that was stationary and the surrounding countryside that was moving.

Mrs Brown had gone into a nursing home for a slight operation, and, in order to relieve the domestic strain, William was being sent to stay with an old school friend of hers, who lived at a small seaside resort called Sea Beach.

He was enjoying the journey. He always enjoyed journeys. He enjoyed the motion and the change from the ordinary routine of life. They had a generally exhilarating effect on him, and he could, of course, enliven them by pretending that he was anyone going anywhere.

Since the journey began he had pretended that he was a spy travelling disguised through an enemy country (none of the other people in the carriage suspected him), a general on his way to the war (the other people in the carriage were his staff), and a circus man travelling with his show (the large man with the long nose was an elephant and the woman in the black satin coat was a performing seal).

All the other passengers had got out at various stations, and now William was alone, pretending to be a wizard, who, by a wave of his wand, made trees, fields, telegraph posts skip to his bidding.

After a few minutes he tired of this; he was growing slightly bored. Suddenly his eye lit on the notice: "To stop the train, pull down the chain."

He stretched out his hand to it, then read: "Penalty for improper use, £5", and, after a hasty mental calculation that assessed his entire capital at the sum of one shilling and sixpence halfpenny, put his hand down again.

But the fascination of it was more than he could resist. He fingered the chain, and imagined himself pulling it. He wondered if it really worked and, if it worked, how it worked. It probably put on a sort of brake. There wouldn't be any harm in just pulling it a tiny bit. That would only just make the train go a little bit more slowly. No one would even notice it.

He pulled the chain an infinitesimal fraction.

Nothing happened.

He pulled it a little harder.

Still nothing happened.

He pulled it harder still. There was a sudden screaming of brakes, and the train drew to an abrupt standstill.

William crouched in his corner of the carriage, frozen with horror. Perhaps, he thought desperately, if he sat quite still and didn't move or breathe, they wouldn't know who'd done it.

The guard came running down by the side of the train. As he approached William's carriage, an elderly, red-faced, military-looking gentleman leant out of the next window, and gasped: "Guard, guard! You're in the nick of time"; then poured out an incoherent story about a man who had demanded money from him, and was just raising his stick to brain him when the train stopped.

"Then, of course, he jumped and escaped," he ended. "Look! There he is!"

The figure of a large but nimble man could be seen disappearing across a field on the other side of the train. Immediately outside the carriage was the stick that he had evidently thrown away in his flight.

"Just in time, guard," panted the military-looking man, mopping his brow. "Another minute, and—"

William heaved a sigh of relief. No one would now know that it was he who had pulled the chain.

"But you didn't pull the chain, sir," the guard was saying.

"No, the brute was standing right over me, so that I couldn't move. He—"

"The chain was pulled from this carriage," went on the guard, moving towards William, who sat in his corner, frozen by horror once more, trying to efface himself against the carriage back.

The guard stood and looked at him for a few seconds in silence, then he said:

"That was smart work of yours, nipper. I suppose, sir," he went on, turning to the military-looking man, "he heard this fellow threatening you and pulled the chain."

William, after a few seconds' complete bewilderment, clutched gratefully at this heaven-sent deliverance.

The military-looking man shook hands with him, thanked him effusively, and gave him a ten shilling note. The other passengers came up and crowded round him,

THE PASSENGERS CROWDED ROUND AND CONGRATULATED HIM.

wringing his hand and congratulating him. An old lady gave him a peppermint drop. A little girl produced an autograph album and asked for his signature.

William, though still somewhat bewildered, assumed an air of modest heroism.

Finally, the guard, having taken all the particulars of his adventure from the military-looking man, sent everyone back to their carriage, and the train started once more on its way.

William, alone in his carriage, felt at first merely a great relief at his providential rescue from ignominy. Then gradually the imaginary scene became more and more real. He saw himself starting up at the sound of a fierce altercation from the next carriage, then coming to a sudden decision and dashing to the chain. He sat for the rest of the journey smiling modestly to himself, bathed in a roseate glow of heroism.

His hostess, Mrs Beacon, met him at the station. She was a large, placid woman who, William decided at once, would probably be amenable but uninteresting. He hoped that she would realise that he was a hero. He meant to lose no time in telling her the story.

But it wasn't even necessary to tell it to her, for it turned out that several of the passengers were coming to Sea Beach, and they crowded round William once more, recounting his exploit to his hostess and congratulating him.

William's modest but heroic smile intensified. He depreciated his exploit with airy gestures.

"Oh, it was nothin'," he said; "it jus' sort o' seemed the only thing to do. It was nothin' at all really."

But Sea Beach didn't appear to think it was nothing at all. There had been a complete dearth of local news for several months, and it seized on William with avidity.

Its local paper sent a reporter to interview him and printed his portrait on its first page under the heading: Our Boy Hero. People pointed him out to each other as he walked along the promenade, wearing his modest but heroic smile.

His hostess prepared specially appetising food for him in order to fortify his nerves after the ordeal through which she supposed them to have passed.

For a whole week William revelled in the limelight, then quite suddenly, as it seemed to him, it was gone. A fresh edition of the local paper had come out announcing that a leading inhabitant had won a bowling-match at Morton-on-the-Water, where he was spending his holidays, and that the Mayor's daughter was preparing to swim the Channel.

Moreover, Miss Arabella Love, a well-known musical comedy actress, had arrived at Sea Beach, and in this welter of new sensations William's exploit was completely forgotten.

William himself, as is usual in such cases, was the last person to realise this. He continued to walk along the promenade, wearing his modest but heroic smile, and it was some time before the fact dawned upon him that no one was watching him or talking about him. They were all watching and talking about Miss Arabella Love – a platinum blonde with a ravishing smile and an apparently inexhaustible wardrobe.

William ceased to depreciate the heroism of his exploit. One cannot indeed depreciate something that is never mentioned. He began to recount his exploit vaingloriously and with many additions. He described how a ferocious ruffian had suddenly begun to threaten him in a railway carriage and how, after a tremendous tussle, he had managed to overpower him and pull the communication cord.

No one but his contempories, however, would listen to him, and his contemporaries, after listening to him, would derisively recount similar exploits of their own. Even his hostess no longer prepared him appetising dishes but began to give him cold beef and rice pudding.

William stopped talking about his train exploit and became very thoughtful. He had tasted the limelight, found it good, and, like Oliver Twist, he wanted more, but he definitely and reluctantly came to the conclusion that, as far as the limelight went, his train adventure was dead.

The only thing to do was to cut his losses and start afresh.

He felt all the bitterness natural to one who has tackled a ferocious ruffian alone and unaided in a railway carriage (he did really remember it like that by now) without winning any lasting gratitude or kudos from his fellows, but he wasn't going to own himself beaten. A hero he was, and a hero he would continue to be, and, if the train exploit didn't stand good any more, he'd find something else.

The world was full of opportunities of heroism. You'd only got to read the papers to see that. Why, he might rescue someone from drowning . . .

The thought of that encouraged him, and he began to haunt the little beach at the fashionable bathing hours.

Miss Arabella Love was always there, dressed in the latest bathing-model, parading to and fro on the beach or paddling in the foam, surrounded by her crowd of admirers. The reporter from the local paper followed her about with his camera and interviewed her at regular intervals on the burning questions of the day. (She thought the League of Nations was "just too cute for words".)

William sat in the shadow of the rocks and watched this scene morosely. Even if he rescued someone from drowning, would it eclipse this horrible woman with the horrible name?

Then the brilliant idea struck him. He'd save *her* from drowning. That surely would give him all the limelight he could desire.

So far her "swimming" had been of a somewhat primitive nature. She had merely splashed about at the edge of the sea, but she'd surely try to swim properly some time or other, and then . . .

William watched and waited, hanging about on the beach in his bathing suit, ready for all emergencies.

And, as everything is supposed to come to him who waits, so to William there came a day when Miss Arabella Love lingered on the beach after most of her circle had gone in to lunch and, as if suddenly weary of posing and paddling, struck out into the open sea.

To William's disappointment, she seemed a fairly good swimmer, but he knew that even good swimmers occasionally get into difficulties, so he continued to watch hopefully from the shore.

Miss Arabella Love was, as a matter of fact, a very good swimmer, and was just learning the "Dolphin Roll". It is not, as practised by a beginner at any rate, a graceful stroke, and so the actress had waited till the coast was clear before she tried it.

Having got well out to sea, she began to practise. She floundered and plunged, and finally disappeared from view.

To William, watching her every movement, it seemed that his desire was at last granted. Miss Arabella Love was in difficulties. His heart leapt exultantly as he struck out from the shore.

He had had no experience in rescuing drowning people, but he thought that it would be easy enough. You just got hold of them and swam back to shore with them.

Miss Love was further out than he had realised, and he was somewhat breathless when he reached her. She was coming to the surface after a particularly strenuous "Dolphin Roll", when she found herself violently clutched at by a small boy.

Miss Arabella Love knew all about life-saving as applied to frantic drowning persons. She freed his hands, ducked him till he was practically unconscious, then swam with him back to the beach.

The news had spread, a crowd had gathered, and the reporter ran up with his camera. A cheer rose as the actress flung her burden upon the sand, and began to pump vigorously at his arms. Finally she said, "He'll be all right now", and, still kneeling by his side, posed for a few more photographs.

Consciousness gradually returned to William. He had been ducked and pummelled ruthlessly, but, being of a robust constitution, had survived it. He sat up on the beach and looked about him. He looked at the sea, then at Miss Love, who stood over him, watching him solicitously. Then he heaved a deep sigh of satisfaction.

He'd rescued her. He must have done or she wouldn't be here. His gaze passed on to the attendant crowd and to the photographer, and he assumed his modest but heroic smile.

"SHE DIDN'T RESCUE ME FROM DROWNING," SAID WILLIAM. "I RESCUED HER. SHE STRUGGLED SOMETHING TERRIBLE."

A tall, thin man stepped forward.

"Well, my boy, aren't you going to thank your rescuer?"

The modest heroic smile died from William's lips.

"My what?" he said hoarsely.

"This lady here," said the man sternly. "Miss Arabella Love. She rescued you from drowning, didn't she?"

"No, she didn't," said William indignantly. "I rescued her."

A roar of laughter answered him.

"But I did," he protested fiercely. "I tell you, I did. I saw her out there drownin', an' I went out an' brought her back. She struggled with me something terrible, but I brought her back all right."

Another roar of laughter greeted this statement.

"Poor little chap!" said an old lady pityingly. "It's affected his brain."

"Come, come, my boy," said the tall, thin man gravely. "A joke's a joke, but that's a very poor one. Thank the lady like a gentleman."

"But I *did* rescue her," William repeated wildly. "You've all made a mistake. I saw her drownin' an' I swam out to her an'—"

At this point Mrs Beacon arrived breathless, having received an exaggerated report of the incident from a friend who said that she had seen Miss Arabella Love wading ashore with William's body in her arms. She was relieved to find him still alive.

"Oh, William!" she panted. "I do wish you'd be more careful."

"But I was; I didn't," said William desperately. "They won't listen to me. It was me that did it. She was—"

"Poor little chap!" said the kind old lady again. "He's delirious. No wonder, considering he's just been at death's door, so to speak. I'd get him home and to bed, my dear, if I were you. Give him something hot to drink."

Mrs Beacon led William away, still loudly and passionately denying his rescue, while Miss Arabella Love, wearing almost exactly the expression of modest heroism that William had so reluctantly discarded, stood in a little circle of admirers and described to the reporter her exact sensation when she felt the frantic clutch of the drowning boy.

The full horror of the situation dawned upon William the next day when, opening the local paper, he saw a large and very flattering photograph of Miss Arabella Love, as the rescuer, and beneath it a small and very unflattering one of himself, as the rescued.

There followed a detailed account of the affair, described by the actress, and a comment on the folly of small boys who venture out of their depth, thus occasioning unnecessary trouble to everyone concerned, ending with a graceful compliment to "our distinguished and highly accomplished visitor".

William went about sunk deep in gloom. So far from being a hero he was now in the ignominious position of having been rescued – he, William – and by a woman with a name like Arabella Love.

To make matters worse, his rescuer adopted a proprietary attitude towards him, patting his head and flashing her ravishing smile at him whenever they met, quite undeterred by his scowls.

He promised himself grimly to let her drown next time, but the promise failed to yield him much comfort.

The worst part of it all was that Mrs Beacon, thinking that his parents would be interested in the incident, had sent a cutting from the local paper to his home. The news would be all over the village by now. All his friends – and what was more important, his enemies – would have heard of it.

He, who had meant to return home as the hero of the

train incident, would have to return to the pitiful rôle of the boy who had been rescued from drowning by Miss Arabella Love. And he couldn't do anything about it. There was only a week before he had to go home, and one couldn't do anything in a week.

Or could one?

His incurable optimism rose to answer the question. One could and one must. William was not the boy to submit tamely to fate. He was a hero, and he must, by some means or other, win back his heroic status.

A brief survey of the situation told him that life-saving was his only hope. He must save someone else from drowning, leaving no doubt in this case as to who was the rescuer, and who was rescued. If he could only do this, he would not only reclaim his position as hero, but also throw strong doubt upon Miss Arabella Love's pretensions to having saved him.

He began to hang about the beach again, wearing his bathing costume, waiting for his services to be required, watching all swimmers, children and adults, with a stern and anxious eye.

The days passed with no result, however, and William continued to fill the ignominious position of "The Boy whom Miss Arabella Love had Rescued".

The last day arrived. Moodily, almost despondently (for even William's optimism had its limits), he wandered to the end of the wooden jetty that ran for some distance out to sea, in order to brood in solitude.

The jetty was deserted except for a large black dog of the Labrador species, who greeted William as a long-lost brother, and began to gambol in puppy fashion round his feet.

Even that failed to raise William's spirits, until, as he gazed down at it, an idea suddenly occurred to him. He looked at the shore. A fair number of people were there – among them, he noticed, the reporter from the local paper.

He went to the edge of the jetty, the dog accompanying him. Then, with a deft movement of his foot, he pushed the dog over the edge, and, flinging up his arms, dived in after it.

He soon found it, held on to it fast, and eventually reached land with it.

Luckily the people on the beach had seen the occurrence. A cheer went up and the reporter took a photograph. William, remembering the success of his modest demeanour over the train incident, merely smiled a deprecating smile and walked homeward.

He said nothing to his hostess. He meant her to remember later that he had said nothing to her. He saw her in imagination reading the glowing account of the rescue in the local press – it was fortunate that tomorrow was the day the local paper came out – and saying: "And he never even mentioned it to anyone. He just came home as if he'd been bathing as usual, and he never said a word to me about saving that dog's life."

The story would travel round the little seaside resort. "You remember that boy who saved the dog's life so pluckily? Well, he never even *mentioned* it when he got home." People would then recall the train exploit. "It was the same boy, you know, who tackled that ruffian in the train so bravely, and was so modest about it."

He was to start home by the first train the next morning. Mrs Beacon prepared an early breakfast for him,

A CHEER WENT UP, AND THE REPORTER TOOK A PHOTOGRAPH.

but he ate it absently, glancing round as if in search of something.

"The paper not come yet?" he said.

"No dear," said Mrs Beacon. "It won't come till after you're gone. Why do you want the paper?"

"Oh, nothing," said William modestly, but he assured himself the news would be even more effective if it arrived after his departure. It would still further emphasise his modesty. ("He actually went home without mentioning it.")

At the station he had just time to buy a paper as the train steamed out. He leant back in his seat, a complacent smile on his lips. He'd show it to all his friends. His reputation as a hero would be made for life. Slowly he opened the page.

Yes, there it was – a picture of himself and the dog side by side. But when his eyes turned to the letterpress the smile died from his lips.

"DOG RESCUES SMALL BOY

"A half-grown pup belonging to Miss Arabella Love today rescued from drowning the same small boy whom Miss Arabella Love herself rescued only a few days ago. We must . . ."

But William read no more.

CHAPTER TWO

AN AFTERNOON WITH WILLIAM

WILLIAM'S FAMILY was staying at the seaside for its summer holidays. This time was generally cordially detested by William. He hated being dragged from his well-known haunts, his woods and fields and friends and dog (for Jumble was not the kind of dog one takes away on a holiday). He hated the uncongenial atmosphere of hotels and boarding houses. He hated the dull promenades and the town gardens where walking over the grass and playing at Red Indians was discouraged. He failed utterly to understand the attraction that such places seemed to possess for his family. He took a pride and pleasure in the expression of gloom and boredom that he generally managed to maintain during the whole length of the holiday. But this time it was different. Ginger was staying with his family in the same hotel as William.

Ginger's father and William's father played golf together. Ginger's mother and William's mother looked at the shops and the sea together. William and Ginger went off together on secret expeditions. Though no cajoleries or coaxings would have persuaded William to admit that he was "enjoying his holiday", still the presence of Ginger made it difficult for him to maintain his usual aspect of gloomy scorn. They hunted for smugglers in the caves, they slipped over seaweedy rocks and fell into the pools left by the retreating tide. They carried on warfare from trenches which they made in the sand, dug mines and counter-mines and generally got damp sand so deeply ingrained in their clothes and hair that, as Mrs Brown said almost tearfully, they "simply defied brushing".

Today they were engaged in the innocent pursuit of wandering along the front and sampling the various attractions which it offered. They stood through three performances of the Punch and Judy show, laughing uproariously each time. As they had taken possession of the best view and as it never seemed to occur to them to contribute towards the expenses, the showman finally ordered them off. They wandered off obligingly and bought two penny sticks of liquorice at the next stall. Then they bought two penny giant glasses of a biliousy-coloured green lemonade and quaffed them in front of the stall with intense enjoyment. Then they wandered away from the crowded part of the front to the empty space beyond the rocks. Ginger found a dead crab and William made a fire and tried to cook it, but the result was not encouraging. They ate what was left of their liquorice sticks to take away the taste, then went on to the caves. They reviewed the possibility of hunting for smugglers without enthusiasm. William was feeling disillusioned with smugglers. He seemed to have spent the greater part of his life hunting for smugglers. They seemed to be an unpleasantly secretive set of people. They might have let him catch just one . . .

They flung stones into the retreating tide and leapt

into the little pools to see how high they could make the splashes go.

Then they saw the boat . . .

It was lying by itself high and dry on the shore. It was a nice little boat with two oars inside.

"Wonder how long it would take to get to France in it?" said William.

"Jus' no time, I 'spect," said Ginger. "Why you can *see* France from my bedroom window. It must jus' be *no* distance – simply *no* distance."

They looked at the boat in silence for a few minutes.

"It looks as if it would go quite easy," said William.

"We'd have it back before whosever it is wanted it," said Ginger.

"We couldn't do it any harm," said William.

"It's simply *no* distance to France from my bedroom window," said Ginger.

The longing in their frowning countenances changed to determination.

"Come on," said William.

It was quite easy to push and pull the boat down to the water. Soon they were seated, their hearts triumphant and their clothes soaked with sea water, in the little boat and were being carried rapidly out to sea. At first William tried to ply the oars but a large wave swept them both away.

"Doesn't really matter," said William cheerfully. "The tide's takin' us across to France all right without botherin' with oars."

For a time they lay back enjoying the motion and trailing fingers in the water.

" 'S almost as good as bein' pirates, isn't it?" said William.

At the end of half an hour Ginger said with a dark frown:

"Seems to *me* we aren't goin' in the right d'rection for France. Seems to *me*, Cap'n, we've been swep' out of our course. I can't see no land anywhere."

"Well, we mus' be goin' *somewhere*," said William the optimist, "an' wherever it is it'll be *int'resting*."

"It *mightn't* be," said Ginger, who was ceasing to enjoy the motion and was taking a gloomy view of life.

"Well, I'm gettin' jolly hungry," said William.

"Well, I'm *not*," said Ginger.

William looked at him with interest.

"You're lookin' a bit pale," he said with over-cheerful sympathy. "P'raps it was the crab."

Ginger made no answer.

"Or it might have been the liquorice *or* the lemonade," said William with interest.

"I wish you'd shut up talking about them," snapped Ginger.

"Well, I feel almost *dyin'* of hunger," said William. "In books they draw lots and then one kills the other an' eats him."

"I wun't mind anyone killin' an' eatin' me," said Ginger.

"I've nothin' to kill you with, anyway, so it's no good talkin' about it," said William.

"Seems to me," said Ginger raising his head from his gloomy contemplation of the waves, "that we keep changin' the d'rection we're goin' in. We'll like as not end at America or China or somewhere."

"An' our folks'll think we're drowned."

"We'll prob'ly find gold mines in China or somewhere an' make our fortunes."

"An' we'll come home changed an' old an' they won't know us."

Their spirits rose.

Suddenly William called excitedly, "I see land! Jus' *look!*"

They were certainly rapidly nearing land.

"Thank goodness," murmured Ginger.

"An uninhabited island I 'spect," said William.

"Or an island inhabited by wild savages," said Ginger.

The boat was pushed gently on to land by the incoming tide.

Ginger and William disembarked.

"I don't care where we are," said Ginger firmly, "but I'm goin' to stop here all my life. I'm not goin' in that ole boat again."

A faint colour had returned to his cheeks.

"You *can't* stop on an uninhabited island all your life," said William aggressively. "You'll *have* to go away. You needn't go an' eat dead crabs jus' before you start, but you can't live on an uninhabited island all your life."

"Oh, do shut up talkin' about dead crabs," said Ginger.

"Here's a hole in a hedge," called William. "Let's creep through and see what there is the other side. Creep, mind, an' don't breathe. It'll prob'ly be wild savages or cannibals or something."

They crept through the hedge.

There in a wide green space some lightly-clad beings

were dancing backwards and forwards. One in the front called out unintellible commands in a shrill voice.

William and Ginger crept behind a tree.

"Savages!" said William in a hoarse whisper. "Cannibals!"

"Crumbs!" said Ginger. "What'll we do?"

The white-clad figures began to leap into the air.

"Charge 'em," said William, his freckled face set in a determined frown. "Charge 'em and put 'em to flight utterin' wild yells to scare 'em – before they've time to know we're here."

"All right," said Ginger, "come on."

"Ready?" said William through set lips. "Steady . . . Go!"

The New School of Greek Dancing was a few miles down the coast from where William and Ginger had originally set forth in the boat. The second afternoon open-air class was in progress. Weedy males and æsthetic-looking females dressed in abbreviated tunics with sandals on their feet and fillets round their hair, mostly wearing horn spectacles, ran and sprang and leapt and gambolled and struck angular attitudes at the shrill command of the instructress and the somewhat unmusical efforts of the (very) amateur flute player.

"Now run . . . *so* . . . hands extended . . . *so* . . . left leg up . . . *so* . . . head looking over shoulder . . . *so* . . . no, try not to overbalance . . . that piece again . . . never mind the music . . . just do as I say . . . *so* . . . *Ow* . . . *OW!*"

"*Go!*"

Two tornadoes rushed out from behind a tree and

WILLIAM AND GINGER RUSHED OUT FROM BEHIND A TREE AND CHARGED WILDLY INTO THE CROWD OF ÆSTHETIC AND BONY REVELLERS.

charged wildly into the crowd of æsthetic and bony revellers. With heads and arms and legs they fought and charged and kicked and pushed and bit. They might have been a dozen instead of two. A crowd of thin, lightly-clad females ran screaming indoors. One young man nimbly climbed a tree and another lay prone in a rose bush.

"We've put 'em to flight," said William breathlessly, pausing a moment from his labours.

"Yes," said Ginger dispiritedly, "an' what'll we do *next?*"

"Oh, jus' keep 'em at bay an' live on their food," said William vaguely, "an' p'raps they'll soon begin to worship us as gods."

But William was unduly optimistic. The flute player

had secured some rope from an outhouse and, accompanied by some other youths, he was already creeping up behind William. In a few moments' time William and Ginger found themselves bound to neighbouring trees. They struggled wildly. They looked a strange couple. The struggle had left them tieless and collarless. Their hair stood on end. Their faces were stained with liquorice juice.

"They'll eat us for supper," said William to Ginger. "Sure's Fate they'll eat us for supper. They're prob'ly boilin' the water to cook us in now. Go on, try'n *bite* through your rope."

"I have tried," said Ginger wearily. "It's nearly pulled my teeth out."

"I wish I'd told 'em to give Jumble to Henry," said William sadly. "They'll prob'ly keep him to themselves or sell him."

"They'll be *sorry* they took my trumpet off me when they hear I'm eaten by savages," said Ginger with a certain satisfaction.

The Greek dancers were drawing near by degrees from their hiding places.

"*Mad!*" they were saying. "One of them *bit* me and he's probably got hydrophobia. I'm going to call on my doctor." "He simply *charged* me in the stomach. I think it's given me appendicitis." "*Kicked* my leg. I can *see* the bruise." "*Quite* spoilt the atmosphere."

"William," said Ginger faintly, "isn't it funny they talk English? Wun't you expect them to talk some savage language?"

"I speck they've learnt it off folks they've eaten."

From the open window of the house behind the trees

came the loud tones of a lady who was evidently engaged in speaking through a telephone.

"Yes, *wild* . . . absolutely *mad* . . . *must* have escaped from the asylum . . . no one escaped from the asylum? . . . then they must have been *going* to the asylum and escaped on the *way* . . . well, if they aren't *lunatics* they're *criminals.* Please send a large *force.*"

It was when two stalwart and quite obviously English policemen appeared that William's bewilderment finally took from him the power of speech.

"Crumbs!" was all he said.

He was quite silent all the way home. He coldly repulsed all the policemen's friendly overtures.

Mrs Brown screamed when from the lounge window she saw her son and his friend approaching with their escort. It was Mr Brown who went boldly out to meet them, paid vast sums of hush money to the police force and brought in his son by the scruff of his neck.

"Well," said William almost tearfully, at the end of a long and painful course of home truths, " 'f they'd reely *been* cannibals and eaten me you'd p'raps have been *sorry.*"

Mr Brown whose peace had been disturbed and reputation publicly laid low by William's escort and appearance, looked at him.

"You flatter yourself, my son," he said with bitterness.

"What'll we do today?" said Ginger the next morning.

"Let's start with watchin' the Punch and Judy," said William.

MR BROWN PAID VAST SUMS OF HUSH MONEY TO THE POLICE FORCE AND BROUGHT IN HIS SON BY THE SCRUFF OF THE NECK.

"I'm not goin' in no boats," said Ginger firmly.

"All right," said William cheerfully, "but if we find another dead crab I've thought of a better way of cooking it."

CHAPTER THREE

THAT BOY

WILLIAM HAD gone away with his family for a holiday, and he was not enjoying it. For one reason it was not the sea. Last summer they had gone to the sea and William had enjoyed it. He had several times been rescued from a watery grave by passers-by. He had lost several pairs of new shoes and stockings by taking them off among the rocks and then roaming so far afield barefoot that he forgot where he had left them and so came home without them. He got wet through every day as a matter of course. Through the house where his family stayed his track was marked by a trail of sand and seaweed and small deceased crabs. He had upon one occasion floated out to sea in a boat which he had found on the beach and loosened from its moorings, and narrowly escaped being run down by a steamer. At the end of the holiday by the sea Mrs Brown had said weakly, "Let it be somewhere inland next year."

William found things monotonous inland. There were no crabs and nothing to do. Robert and Ethel, his grown-up brother and sister, had joined a tennis club and were out all day. Not that William had much use for Robert and Ethel. He preferred them out all day as a matter of fact.

"All I say *is*," he said aggrievedly to his mother, "that

no one cares whether I'm havin' a nice time or not. You think that s'long as father can go golfin' – or *tryin'* to golf – and those two playin' tennis – or what they *call* tennis" – he added scornfully, "and you can sit knittin', it's all *right*. You don't think of *me*. No one thinks of me. I might just as well not be here. All I say *is*," he ended, "I might jus' as well be *dead* for all the trouble some people take to make me happy."

His mother looked at his scowling freckled countenance.

"Well, dear," she said, "there are plenty of books about the house that you haven't read."

"*Books*," said William scornfully. "Sir Walter Scott's ole things – I don't call that *books*."

"You can go for walks."

"*Walks!*" said William. "It's no use goin' walks without Jumble."

His father lowered his newspaper. "Your arithmetic report was vile," he said. "You might occupy your time with a few sums. I'll set them for you."

William turned upon his parent a glance before which most men would have quailed. Even William's father, inured as he was by long experience to that glare of William's, retired hastily behind his paper. Then, with a short and bitter laugh, William turned on his heel and left the room. That was the last straw. He'd finished with them. He'd simply finished with them.

He put his head in at the window as he went towards the gate.

"I'm goin' out, mother," he said in a voice which expressed stern sorrow rather than anger.

"All right, dear," said Mrs Brown sweetly.

"I may not be coming back – never," he added darkly.

"All right, dear," said William's mother.

William walked with slow dignity down to the gate.

"All I say *is*," he remarked pathetically to the gatepost as he passed, "I might as well be *dead* for all anyone thinks of tryin' to make my life a bit happier."

He walked down to the village – a prey to black dejection. What people came away for holidays *for* beat him. At home there was old Jumble to take for a walk and throw sticks for, and the next-door cat to tease and the butcher's boy to fight, and various well-known friends and enemies to make life interesting. Here there was . . . Well, all he said *was*, he might as well be *dead*.

A charabanc stood outside the post office, and people were taking their places in it. William looked at it contemptuously. He began to listen in a bored fashion to the conversation of two young men.

"I'm awfully glad you ran down," one of them was saying to the other; "we can have a good tramp together. To tell you the truth I'd got so bored that I'd taken a ticket for this charabanc show . . . Can't stand 'em really."

"Will they give you your money back?" said the other.

"It doesn't matter," said the first.

Then he met William's dark, unflinching gaze and said carelessly, "Here, kid, like a ticket for the charabanc trip?"

William considered the question. Anything that would take him away from the immediate vicinity of his family seemed at that moment desirable.

"Does it come back?" he said.

"It's *supposed* to," said the young man.

That seemed rather a drawback. William felt that he

would have preferred to go away from his family on something that did not come back. However, this was better than nothing.

"All right," he said graciously, "I don't mind going."

The young man handed him the ticket.

William sat in the middle of a seat between a very fat lady and a very fat gentleman.

"Not much *room*," he remarked bitterly to the world in general.

The fat lady and the fat gentleman turned crushing glances upon him simultaneously. William received and returned them. He even enlarged upon his statement.

"All I say *is*," he said pugnaciously, trying to scowl up at both sides at once, "that there's not much *room*."

The fat lady put up lorgnettes and addressed the fat gentleman over William's head.

"What a very rude little boy!" she said.

Being apparently agreed upon that point they became friendly and conversed together for the rest of the journey, ignoring the subterranean rumbles of indignation that came from the small boy between them.

At last the charabanc stopped at a country village. The driver explained that the church was an excellent example of Early Norman architecture. This left William cold. He did not even glance at it. The driver went on to remark that an excellent meal could be obtained at the village inn. Here William's expression kindled into momentary animation only to fade again into despair. For William had spent his last twopence that morning upon a stick of liquorice. It had caused a certain amount of fric-

"ALL I SAY *IS*," WILLIAM SAID PUGNACIOUSLY, TRYING TO SCOWL UP AT BOTH SIDES AT ONCE, "THAT THERE'S NOT MUCH *ROOM*."

tion between himself and his elder brother. William had put it – partially sucked – upon a chair while he went to wash his hands, and Robert had come in from tennis and inadvertently sat down upon it. Being in a moist condition it had adhered to Robert's white flannel trousers. Even when detached the fact of its erstwhile adherence could not be concealed. William had considered Robert's attitude entirely unreasonable.

"Well, I don't know what he's got to be mad about . . . I didn't make him sit down on it, did I? He talks about me spoilin' his trousers – well, wot about him spoilin' my liquorice? All I say *is* – who wants to eat it, now he's been sittin' on it?"

Robert had unkindly taken this statement at its face value and thrown the offending stick of liquorice into the fire.

William sadly extricated himself from the charabanc, thinking bitterly of the vanished twopence, and liquorice, and the excellent meal to be obtained from the village inn. He regarded himself at that moment as a martyr whose innocence and unjust persecution equalled that of any in the pages of the Church History book.

An elderly lady in pince-nez looked at him pityingly.

"What's the matter, little boy?" she said. "You look unhappy."

William merely smiled bitterly.

"Is your mother with you?" she went on.

"Nope," said William, thrusting his hands into his pockets and and scowling still more.

"Your father, then?"

"Huh!" said William, as though bitterly amused at the idea.

"You surely haven't come alone!" said the lady.

William gave vent to the dark emotions of his soul.

"All I say *is*," he said, "that if you knew my family you'd be jolly glad to go anywhere alone if you was me."

The lady made little clicking noises with her tongue expressive of sorrow and concern.

"Dear, dear, dear!" she said. "And are you going to have tea now?"

William assumed his famous expression of suffering patience.

"I've got no money. It's not much use goin' to have tea anywhere when you haven't got no money."

"Haven't they given you any money for your tea?" said the lady indignantly.

"Not *they!*" said William with a bitter laugh. "*They* wun't of let me come if they'd known. *They* wun't of paid anything for me. It was a frien' gave me the ticket jus' to giv' me a bit of pleasure," he said pathetically, "but *they* wun't even give me money for my tea."

"Perhaps," said the lady, "you had a late lunch and they thought—"

"Huh!" ejaculated William. "I din' have *any* lunch worth speakin' of." He thrust aside the mental picture of two helpings of steak and three of rice pudding.

"You *poor* child," said the lady. "Come along, *I'll* give you your tea."

"Thanks," said William humbly and gratefully, trudging off with her in the direction of the village inn.

He felt torn between joy at the immediate prospect of a meal and pity for his unhappy home life. William, generally speaking, had only to say a thing to believe it. He saw himself now as the persecuted victim of a cruel and unsympathetic family, and the picture was not without a certain pleasure. William enjoyed filling the centre of the stage in any capacity whatsoever.

"I suppose," said the lady uncertainly, as William consumed boiled eggs with relish, "that your family are *kind* to you."

"You needn't s'pose that," said William, his mouth full of bread-and-butter, his scowling gaze turned on her lugubriously. "You jus' needn't s'pose that. Not with *my* family."

"They surely aren't *cruel* to you?" said the lady in horror.

"*Crule*," said William with a shudder, "jus' isn't the word. All I say *is*, crule isn't the word."

The lady leant across the table.

"Little boy," she said soulfully, "you must tell me *all*. I want to *help* you. I go about the world helping people, and I'm going to help you. Don't be frightened. You know people can be put in prison for being cruel to children. If I reported the case to the Society for Prevention of Cruelty to Children—"

William was slightly taken back.

"Oh, I wun't like you to do that!" he said hastily. "I wun't like to get them into trouble."

"Ah," she said, "but you must think of your happiness, not theirs!"

She watched, fascinated, as William finished a third plate of bread-and-butter, and yet his hunger seemed to be unappeased. She was not acquainted with the digestive capacity of an average healthy boy of eleven.

"I can see you've been starved," she said, "and I could tell at once from your expression that you were unhappy. Have you any brothers and sisters?"

William, who had now reached the second stage of his tea, put half a cake into his mouth, masticated and swallowed it before replying.

"Two," he said briefly, "one each. Grown up. But they jus' care nothin' but their own pleasure. Why," he went on, warming to his theme, "this morning I bought a few sweets with jus' a bit of money I happened to have, an' he took them from me and threw them into the fire. Jus' threw them into the fire."

"LITTLE BOY," SHE SAID SOULFULLY, "YOU MUST TELL ME ALL . . . IF I REPORTED THE CASE TO THE SOCIETY FOR PREVENTION OF CRUELTY TO CHILDREN—"

The lady made the sympathetic clicking sound with her tongue.

"Dear! Dear! Dear!" she said again. "How very unkind!"

William somewhat reluctantly refused the last piece of cake. He had, as a matter of fact, done full justice to the excellent meal provided by the village inn. It had given him a feeling of gentle, contented melancholy. He was basking in the thought of his unhappy home life.

"I'm sorry to keep reminding you of it," said the lady, "but I feel I really want to get to the bottom of it. There's generally only one explanation of an unhappy home. I've investigated so many cases. Does your father drink?"

William nodded sadly.

"Yes," he said. "That's it."

"Oh," breathed the lady, "your *poor* mother!"

But William wanted no division of sympathy.

"Mother drinks, too," he said.

"You *poor*, poor child!" said the lady.

William wondered whether to make Robert and Ethel drink, too, then decided not to. As an artist he knew the value of restraint.

"Never mind," said the lady, "you shall have *one* happy afternoon, at any rate."

She took him to the village shop and bought him chocolates, and sweets, and bananas, and a top. William found some difficulty in retaining an expression suggestive of an unhappy home life, but he managed it fairly successfully.

He began to feel very sleepy on the way home. He had had a lovely time. His pockets were full of sweets and chocolates, and he held his top in his hand. He even felt that he could forgive his family. He'd heap coals of fire on Robert's head by giving him a chocolate . . . He was almost asleep when the charabanc drew up at the post office. Everyone began to descend. He took a polite and distant farewell of the elderly lady and set off for his home. But he found that the elderly lady was coming with him.

"Where do you live?" she said.

"Oh," said William vaguely, "jus' somewhere along here."

"I'm coming to see your father," said the lady in a determined voice.

William was aghast.

"Oh – er – I wun't do that if I was you!" he said.

"I often find," she said, "that a drunkard does not realise what unhappiness he makes in his home. I often find that a few words of warning are taken to heart—"

"You'd better *not*," said William desperately. "He dun't mind *wot* he does! He'd throw knives at you or shoot you or cut your head off soon as not. He'll be jus' mad drunk when we get in. He went off to the public house jus' after breakfast. You'd better not come *near* our house . . . All I say *is*, you might jus' as well be *dead* as coming to our house."

"But what about you?"

"Oh, I'm used to it," said William valiantly. "I don't mind. Please, you'd better not come," he urged. "I'm thinkin' of *you*—"

"I shan't feel that I've done my duty till I've at any rate tried to make him see his sin."

They were in the street now in which William's family were living. William looked pale and desperate. Matters seemed to have gone beyond his control. Suddenly he had an idea. He would lead her past the house and on and on till one or other of them dropped from fatigue. She'd have to go home some time. She couldn't go on all night. He could say he'd forgotten where he lived. He began to dislike her intensely. Fussy ole thing! Believing everything everyone said to her! Interfering with other people's drunken fathers! He was creeping cautiously and silently past his house by the side of his unsuspecting companion, when a shrill cry reached him.

"William! Hi! William! Where have you been? Mother says come in at once!"

It was Ethel leaning out of an upstairs window. The

sight of her pretty white-clad figure brought no pleasure to her brother's heart. He put out his tongue at her and sadly opened the garden gate.

"You'd better not come in," he said faintly to his companion, in a last feeble attempt to avert the catastrophe which Fate seemed determined to bring upon him, "he gets *vi'lent* about this time of day."

With firm set lips his companion followed him.

"I must do my *duty*," she said sternly.

Mr Brown looked up from the evening paper as his younger son entered. At first he merely noticed that his younger son looked unusually sheepish. Then he noticed that his son was followed by a tall, thin lady of prim appearance and uncertain age, wearing pince-nez. Mr Brown groaned inwardly. Had William killed her cat or merely broken one of her windows?

"Er – good evening," he said.

"Good evening," said the visitor. "I have been spending the afternoon with your little boy."

Mr Brown sent William a speaking glance. He didn't mind what characters William picked up outside the house, but he wished he'd keep them there. William refused to meet his father's glance. He sat on the edge of a chair looking rather pale, his cap in his hand, measuring with his eye the distance between the chair and the half-open door.

"Very kind of you," murmured Mr Brown.

"He has told me something of the state of things in his home," burst out the visitor. "I saw at once that he was unhappy and half-starved."

Mr Brown's jaw dropped. William very slowly and cautiously tiptoed to the door.

"He told me about you and his mother. I was sure – I am sure – that you don't realise what you are doing – what your – er – failing – means to this innocent child."

Mr Brown raised a hand to his brow.

"Your conscience, you see," said the visitor triumphantly, "troubles you. Why should the memory of childhood mean to that dear boy blows and curses and unkindness – and just because you are a slave to your baser appetites?"

Mr Brown removed his hand from his brow.

"You'll pardon my interrupting you," he said feebly, "but perhaps you would be good enough to give me some slight inkling of what you are talking about."

"Ah, you *know*," she said fervently, "in your soul – in your conscience – you know! Why pretend to me? I have had that dear child's company all afternoon and know what he has suffered." Here Mrs Brown entered and the visitor turned to her. "And you," she went on, "you must be his mother. Can't you – won't you – give it up for the sake of your child?" Her voice quivered with emotion.

"I think, my dear," said Mr Brown, "that you had better send for a doctor. This lady is not well."

"But who *is* she?" said Mrs Brown.

"I don't know," said her husband; "she's someone William found."

The someone William found flung out her arms.

"Won't you?" she cried eloquently. "Can't you – for the sake of your own happiness as well as his – give it up?"

They stared at her.

"Madam," said Mr Brown despairingly, "what do you wish us to give up?"

"*Drink*," she answered dramatically.

Mr Brown sat down heavily.

"*Drink!*" he echoed.

Mrs Brown gave a little scream.

"*Drink!*" she said. "But we're both teetotallers."

It was the turn of the visitor to sit down heavily.

"Surely," she said, "that boy did not deceive me!"

"Madam," said that boy's father bitterly, "it is more than probable."

When the visitor, protesting, apologising, expostulating, and still not quite convinced, had been escorted to the door and seen off the premises, Mr Brown turned grimly to his wife.

"Now," he said, "where is that boy?"

But a long and energetic search of house and garden failed to reveal any traces of him. It was not till an hour later that William, inspired more by the pangs of hunger than by pangs of conscience, emerged from the boot cupboard in the kitchen and surrendered himself to justice.

CHAPTER FOUR

THE CURE

BREAKFAST WAS not William's favourite meal. With his father shut off from the world by his paper, and his mother by her letters, one would have thought that he would have enjoyed the clear field thus left for his activities. But William liked an audience – even a hostile one consisting of his own family. True, Robert and Ethel, his elder brother and sister, were there; but Robert's great rule in life was to ignore William's existence. Robert would have preferred not to have had a small, freckled, snub-nosed brother. But as Fate had given him such a brother, the next best thing was to pretend that he did not exist. On the whole, William preferred to leave Robert alone. And Ethel was awful at breakfast – quite capable of summoning the Head of the Family from behind his *Daily Telegraph* when William essayed a little gentle teasing. This morning William, surveying his family in silence in the intervals of making a very hearty meal, came to the conclusion, not for the first time, that they were hardly worthy of him: Ethel, thinking she was so pretty in that stuck-up-looking dress, and grinning over that letter from that soft girl. Robert talking about football and nobody listening to him, and glaring at him (William) whenever he tried to tell him what nonsense he was talking about it. No, it *wasn't* rounders he was thinking of – he knew 'bout football, thank you, he just did. His mother – suddenly his mother put down her letter.

"Great-Aunt Jane's very ill," she said.

There was a sudden silence. Mr Brown's face appeared above the *Daily Telegraph.*

"Um?" he said.

"Great-Aunt Jane's very ill," said Mrs Brown. "They don't seem to think there's much chance of her getting better. They say . . ." She looked again at the letter as if to make quite sure: "They say she wants to see William. She's never seen him, you know."

There was a gasp of surprise.

Robert voiced the general sentiment.

"Good Lord!" he said, "fancy anyone wanting to see *William*!"

"When they're dying, too," said Ethel in equal horror. "One would think they'd like to die in peace, anyway."

"It hardly seems fair," went on Robert, "to show William to anyone who's not strong."

William glared balefully from one to the other.

"Children! Children!" murmured Mrs Brown.

"How," said Mr Brown, "are you going to get William over to Ireland?"

"I suppose," said Mrs Brown, "that someone must take him."

"Good Lord! Who?"

"Yes, who?" echoed the rest of the family.

"I can't possibly leave the office for the next few weeks," said Mr Brown hastily.

"I simply couldn't face the crossing alone – much less with William," said Ethel.

"I've got my finals coming off next year," said Robert. "I don't want to waste any time. I'm working rather hard these vacs."

"No one," said his father politely, "would have noticed it."

"I can go alone, *thank* you," said William with icy dignity.

In the end William and Mrs Brown crossed to Ireland together.

"If William drops overboard," was Robert's parting shot, "don't worry."

The crossing was fairly eventful. William, hanging over the edge of the steamer, overbalanced, and was rescued from a watery grave by one of the crew who caught him by his trousers as the overbalancing occurred. William was far from grateful.

"Pullin' an' tuggin' at me," he said, "an' I was all right. I was only jus' lookin' over the edge. I'd have got back all right."

But the member of the crew made life hideous to Mrs Brown.

"You know, lady," he muttered, "when I saved yer little boy's life, I give myself such a wrench. I can feel it in my innards now, as it were—"

Hastily she gave him ten shillings. Yet she could not stem the flow.

"I 'ope, lady," he would continue at intervals, "when that choild's growd to be a man, you'll think sometoimes of the poor ole man wot saved 'is life at the expense of 'is own innards, as you might say when 'e were a little 'un."

A speech like that always won half-a-crown. In the end Mrs Brown spent her time avoiding him and fleeing whenever she saw him coming along the deck. When a meeting was inevitable she hastily gave him the largest coin she could find before he could begin on his "innards".

Meanwhile a passenger had discovered William neatly balanced through a porthole, and earned his undying hatred by hauling him in and depositing him upside down on the floor.

"Seems to me," said William to his mother, "that all these folks have come for is to stop other folks having a good time. What do you come on a boat for if you can't look at the sea – that's all I want to know?"

A gale rose, and Mrs Brown, pale and distraught, sat huddled up on deck. William hovered round sympathetically.

"I got some chocolate creams in my other coat. Like some of them?"

"William, dear, don't bother to stay here. I'd just as soon you went away and played."

"Oh no," said William nobly. "I wun't leave you feelin' bad."

The boat gave a lurching heave. Mrs Brown groaned.

"Think you goin' to *be* sick, mother?" said William with interest.

"I – I don't know . . . Wouldn't you like to go over to the other side for a change?"

William wandered away. Soon he returned, holding in his hands two doughnuts – masses of yellowy, greasy-looking dough, bearing the impress of William's grimy fingers.

SOON WILLIAM RETURNED, HOLDING IN HIS HANDS TWO DOUGHNUTS.

"I've got us one each," said William cheerfully. "You must be awful hungry, mother."

Mrs Brown gave one glance and turned towards the sea.

*

In Great-Aunt Jane's drawing room were assembled Uncle John and Aunt Lucy and Cousin Francis. Francis was about the same age as William, but inordinately fat and clad in white. He had fair curls and was the apple of his parents' eyes. They had heard of William but none of them had seen him. There was a murmur of excitement as the sound of the taxi was heard, then William and his mother entered. Mrs Brown was still pale. William followed her, scowling defiantly at the world in general.

"If you have any brandy . . ." said Mrs Brown faintly.

"Brandy?" said William cheerfully. "I never thought of that. I got you nearly everything else, didn't I? I wanted to tempt her to eat," he explained to the company. "I thought of choc'lates an' cakes an' cocoa an' pork pies – I *kept* askin' her to try pork pie – there was some lovely ones on the boat – but I never thought of brandy. Have a good drink of it, mother," he encouraged her, "an' then try an' have a go at the chocolates."

Mrs Brown shivered slightly and sipped the brandy.

"This, William," said Aunt Lucy, "is your cousin Francis."

Cousin Francis held out his hand. "How do you do, William?"

William took the proffered hand. "How do you do?" he said loudly, and added *sotto voce*, "Fatty."

Thus was war declared.

Mrs Brown was feeling better.

"How is Great-Aunt Jane?" she said.

"Sinking," said Uncle John in a voice of deepest gloom. "Sinking fast – sinking fast."

William's expression grew animated.

"Where is she?" he said. "Is she out in the sea?"

"Little boys," said Uncle John still gloomily, "should be seen and not heard."

At this point the nurse entered.

"She can see the little boy now," she said, "if he's come."

"Let the dear children go together," suggested Aunt Lucy.

"Excellent," said Uncle John in his hushed, sepulchral voice. "Excellent – together."

William and Francis went upstairs behind the nurse.

The bedroom was large and dim. At the far end lay Great-Aunt Jane, propped up in a high old-fashioned bed. The nurse took them across.

"I only wanted to see William," said Great-Aunt Jane feebly. "The other need not have come. So this is Margaret's youngest, is it? I've seen the others, Robert and Ethel. But I hadn't seen this one. I didn't want to die without seeing all my family. He's not as beautiful as Francis, but he's less fat. Do you trail clouds of glory, William? Francis trails clouds of glory."

"Clouds of fat more like," said William, who was beginning to be bored by the whole affair. Great-Aunt Jane closed her eyes.

"I'm going to rest a little," she said. "You can stay here and get me anything I want while nurse goes to have her tea."

The nurse went.

Great-Aunt Jane fell asleep.

William and Francis were left alone in the dim bedroom, sitting on chairs, one on each side of the big bed as the nurse had placed them. The silence grew oppressive. William fidgeted, then opened hostilities.

"Hello, Fatty!" he whispered over Great-Aunt Jane's recumbent form.

" 'F you call me that again," whispered Francis, "I'll tell my mother."

" 'F you went telling tales of me, I'd pull your long hair off."

Francis searched in his mind, silent for a few minutes, for a suitable term of opprobrium.

"Freckles!" he hissed across the bed at last.

"Softy!" returned William.

This was warfare after his own heart.

" 'F I got hold of you I could throw you out of the window."

"You couldn't. You'd just roll about. You couldn't throw anything. You're too fat."

"I told you what I'd do if you called me that again."

"Tell-tale! Tell-tale! Silly ole tell-tale!"

Still the deadly insults were being hurled across the bed in whispers, and still Great-Aunt Jane slept.

"I could bash your old freckled face in," whispered Francis.

"I could knock your ole long-haired head off."

"I could pull your ears out."

"Come on, then. Have a try."

"Come on yourself!"

Worked up to fighting pitch, they stole round their corners of the bed to the open space at the foot. Then they hurled themselves upon each other.

They fought with fierce satisfaction, tearing at each other's hair, punching each other's heads, squirming and rolling on the floor. Suddenly they became aware of a spectator. Great-Aunt Jane was sitting up in bed, her cheeks flushed, her eyes bright.

"Go it, William!" she said. "Get one in on his nose. That's right, Fatty; well fended! Go on, William. Another, another! No biting, Fatty. Go – Oh, dear!"

There were footsteps on the stairs.

"Quick!" said Great-Aunt Jane.

"GO IT, WILLIAM!" GREAT-AUNT JANE CRIED . . . ! "ANOTHER, ANOTHER!" . . .

They darted to their seats, smoothing their hair as they went.

The nurse entered.

"Whatever . . ." she began, then looked round the peaceful room. "Oh, it must have been in the street!"

Great-Aunt Jane opened her eyes.

"I feel much better," she said. "*Ever* so much better."

"You *look* better," said the nurse. "I hope the children were good."

"Good as gold!" said Great-Aunt Jane, with the ghost of a wink at William.

"Look at them," said the nurse, smiling. "Both purple in the face with holding their breaths. They'd better go now."

Again Great-Aunt Jane winked at William. Downstairs Uncle John was standing, gloomy as ever, by the fireplace.

"How is she?" he said, as they entered.

"I think she's risin' a bit," said William.

"What did you say he did this morning?" said Great-Aunt Jane to the nurse.

"He got up early," said the nurse, "and found a mouse in the mousetrap. He put it into a cardboard box and almost covered the creature in cheese, and made holes in the lid and put it into his pocket. He wanted to keep it. Then the thing gnawed its way out at breakfast and stampeded the whole table. It ran over Francis, and he yelled, and his father nearly fainted. William was much annoyed. He said he'd meant to teach it tricks."

"It was yesterday, wasn't it," said Great-Aunt Jane,

"that he dared Fatty to walk on the edge of the rain tub, and he overbalanced and fell in?"

"Yes – and Fatty got in a temper and bit him, and they fought and rolled down the bank together into the pond."

"And Tuesday—"

"Tuesday he brought the scarecrow in from the field in the evening and put it in front of the fire where his uncle usually stands, and it was rather dark, and they hadn't lit up yet, and his aunt came in and talked to it for quite a long time before she discovered. She's rather short-sighted, you know."

"There was a terrible scuffle going on somewhere last night," said Great-Aunt Jane eagerly.

"Oh, yes – his Uncle John went downstairs about eleven for a book he'd forgotten, and William heard him and thought he was a burglar, and attacked him from behind. They fell downstairs on top of each other, and then William got his uncle rolled up in the hall rug with a pair of gloves in his mouth and his eyeglasses broken before he found out who he was – he's a curious boy!"

Great-Aunt Jane was sitting up and looking quite bright.

"He certainly lends an interest to life. I feel ever so much better since he came. You might send him up now, if he's in, nurse, will you?"

On her way down the nurse met Uncle John.

"How long is this young ruffian going to be here?" he said furiously. William had successfully dispelled the air of hallowed gloom from the house. "He's sent my nerves to pieces already – what his effect on that poor sufferer must be—"

"THERE WAS A TERRIBLE SCUFFLING GOING ON SOMEWHERE, LAST NIGHT."

"He seems to be strengthening *hers*," said the nurse. "She's just sent for him."

"That means a few minutes' peace for the rest of the house, at any rate," he said.

William entered the sickroom sullenly. He was thoroughly bored with life. Even his enemy, Fatty, was not to be found. Fatty retired every afternoon with his mother to lie down.

"Good afternoon, William," said Great-Aunt Jane, "are you enjoying your visit?"

"Well," said William vaguely, striving to temper truth with politeness, "I wun't mind going home now. I've had enough." He sat down on her bed and became confidential. "We've been here for weeks an' weeks—"

"Four days," amended Great-Aunt Jane.

"Well, four days, then," said William, "an' there's nothing left to do, an' they make a fuss if I make a noise; an' I've got a lizard in a box at home and I'm tryin' to teach it tricks, an' it'll have forgot me if I stay here much longer. It was just gettin' to know me. I could tell by its eyes. An' they might forget to feed it or *anything* – there's nothing to *do* here, an' mother's not been well since the sea made her sick, an' I keep sayin' – why wait till she's all right to go back – case the sea makes her sick again; better go back while she's feelin' bad and get it all over again without the fuss of gettin' all right an' then gettin' bad again; an' I keep sayin', *why* are we stoppin' here and stoppin' here an' stoppin' here – an' everyone sayin' '*Sh*!' when you make a noise, or sing, or anything. I say – *why*?"

Great-Aunt Jane's sunken lips were quivering, her eyes twinkling.

"And why are you stoppin' an' stoppin' an' stoppin?'

"She says 'cause you're not out of danger, and we must stop till we know which way it is. Well," he waxed still more confidential, "what I say is, shurely you *know* which way you're goin' to be. Can't you tell us? Then if you're goin' to get better we'll go, an' if you're not—"

"Yes, what then?" said Great-Aunt Jane.

"Then we'll go, too. You don't want me hangin' round when you're dyin'," he said coaxingly. "I'd like as not make a noise, or something, and disturb you – and that lizard might have got out if I go waitin' here much more – like wot that mouse did."

Great-Aunt Jane drew a deep breath of utter content.

"You're too priceless to be true, William," she said.

"Can't you tell me which way?" said William ingratiatingly.

"Yes," said Great-Aunt Jane, "I'm going to get better."

"Oh, crumbs!" he said joyfully. "Can I go and tell mother to pack?"

"You've turned the corner," said the doctor to Great-Aunt Jane an hour later, "we needn't worry about you any more. All these relations of yours can pack up and go."

"William's packed already," said the nurse. "That boy is a cure!"

Great-Aunt Jane laughed.

"Yes, he's a cure, all right," she said.

CHAPTER FIVE

WILLIAM AND THE BUGLE

WILLIAM HAD not joined his School Historical Society because he was fond of history, but because he had heard that the members would be allowed to miss afternoon school on the day of their termly expedition. He realised, of course, that the expedition might be even more boring than afternoon school, but at any rate it would be a change. William liked changes. No one could ever accuse him of getting into a rut.

The history master did not receive his application for membership with enthusiasm.

He knew William only slightly, but what little he knew had not inspired him with any desire to extend the acquaintance. He was a quiet, well-conducted man, passionately interested in history, and he liked quiet, well-conducted boys passionately interested in history. He knew that William was neither quiet nor well-conducted or passionately interested in history.

Still, William had applied for admission to the Society, and he felt that he had no adequate grounds for refusing him, though he decided grimly to stand no nonsense and to eject him on the first excuse.

The Autumn Term expedition was to be made to an

Elizabethan manor house whose grounds contained several Roman remains. William heard this unmoved. He was not interested in Elizabethan manor houses, nor was he interested in Roman remains. He was much relieved, however, by the discovery that he would miss an arithmetic lesson by taking part in the expedition. The arithmetic master shared something of his relief.

But when the day came he was feeling far from cheerful. A friend of Robert's had been over the afternoon before. Like all Robert's friends he had been distant and unbending in his manner to William, and it was quite by accident that William discovered he was a kind of super scout (his official designation was a Rover) and that he possessed a bugle. He had even brought a bugle with him, though he did not perform on it. He had brought it with him in order to give it into Robert's keeping for two days while his own family was removing.

"Things get lost, you know," he explained, "and I shouldn't like anything to happen to it. It's rather a good little bugle."

This had happened the day before the day of the expedition, and on the afternoon of the expedition Robert had gone out, leaving the bugle in the top drawer of his dressing table among his collars and handkerchiefs. William knew that it was there, because he had watched through the keyhole to see where Robert put it. He dared not have entered the room, of course, while Robert was in the house, but this afternoon – the afternoon of the expedition – Robert had gone to tea and supper with a friend who lived in the next village but one. William had been longing to try his hand at the bugle ever since he heard of its existence, and it seemed the irony of fate that it should be left unguarded the very afternoon that he would be away on the Historical Society's expedition.

William, however, was not the boy to sit down meekly and accept the irony of fate. After all, he might be glad of something to relieve the monotony of the Historical Society's expedition, and what more suitable to relieve the monotony of anything than a bugle? Robert would be out of the house before he started for the expedition and would not return till after he was in bed. Robert would leave the bugle safely in his drawer among his collars and handkerchiefs, and find it safely there on his return. No harm would be done to anyone. William did not even intend to use the bugle as a means of annoying the history master. He intended to be very careful indeed, especially as the history master had never yet been known to return any confiscated article to its owner. He did not intend to blow one note upon the instrument. He merely intended to flourish it, to swagger with it, to raise it to his lips for imaginary blasts, to pose before his friends and enemies as the Boy who Possessed a Bugle. He felt that it would be a secret consolation for whatever rigours of boredom the expedition might have in store for him.

The history master – whose name was Mr Perkins, and who was known familiarly as ole Warbeck – eyed him with disfavour when he found him waiting with the other members of the Historical Society at the appointed meeting place. Though he wished the boy no real ill, he had hoped that he would have been prevented – by, say, a slight cold – from coming on the expedition.

William met his gaze with a look of bland innocence, holding the bugle well concealed beneath his coat. The charabanc arrived, and the members scrambled on to it. Mr Perkins sat on the front seat next to Blinks Major, the Secretary of the Society, a thin earnest boy with spectacles, who knew all the dates in English history, and had asked his father for a book on Roman Britain for his last birthday present. William sat on the back seat and drew his bugle from its hiding place.

Mr Perkins, discussing hypocausts with Blinks Major, turned round, frowning, at the sound of hiliarious mirth from the back of the charabanc. William sat gazing dreamily in front of him, surrounded by giggling neighbours. Mr Perkins glared at him suspiciously, then turned round, and resumed his discussion with Blinks Major.

"There's an excellent example of the hypocaust at Northleigh Villa," he said, "but—" Again the sound of uproarious mirth made him frown and turn round quickly. Not quite quickly enough, however. Again William was gazing dreamily in front of him, apparently unaware of the uproar around. He returned to Blinks Major and the discussion upon hypocausts. Again the uproar broke out. Again he wheeled round – just too late.

He could not know, of course, that as soon as his back was turned William raised the bugle to his lips, and with exaggeratedly puffed-out cheeks blew imaginary blasts upon it. It does not take much to amuse small boys in holiday mood, and William was flattered and raised a trifle above himself by the appreciation accorded to his performance. Trying to outdo all his previous efforts, he drew in his breath and – inadvertently let it out with his lips upon the instrument. A loud and inharmonious blast rent the air. Mr Perkins wheeled round. William had been too much surprised to move. Mr Perkins's face went as red as William's.

"Give that to me, Brown," he said sternly.

William handed the offending instrument up to the front seat. Mr Perkins put it with some difficulty into his overcoat pocket.

"And you needn't ask me for it back," he went on, grimly, "because you won't get it."

"He'll have to give it me back," said William apprehensively to his neighbour. "It doesn't belong to me."

"Well, he won't," his neighbour assured him with relish. "He's never given anythin' back that he's taken away. He wouldn't even give Timpkins his watch back that his grandmother had given him the day before. His father went an' made an awful fuss, but he wouldn't."

William, of course, knew that this was true. His mind went fearfully to Robert. Robert would return tonight and find the bugle that had been entrusted into his keeping vanished. There would ensue a scene – or rather a series of scenes – of which William hardly dared to think. Robert, his father, his mother, Robert's friend, seemed to tower above him like outraged giants thirsting for vengeance – Robert, most of all, for Robert would feel that his friend's trust in him had been betrayed, and his wounded honour would seek outlet in exacting the utmost penalty from William. A faint hope that the blame of the vanished bugle could be laid upon burglars was dismissed as soon as it arose. No one would have the slightest doubt as to who had taken the bugle from Robert's drawer. His schoolfellows, in any case, would be sure to spread the news. William looked wistfully at the mouth of the bugle that protruded from Mr Perkins's pocket. It

A LOUD AND INHARMONIOUS BLAST RENT THE AIR.

would probably be easy enough to extract it in the course of the day, but that would not solve the problem. Mr Perkins would have no doubt as to who had removed it and would take immediate steps to secure its return. No, there seemed no solution of the problem that he could see . . .

He dismounted gloomily from the charabanc and inspected with grim disfavour the grey stone walls of the ancient castle.

"Huh!" he said scornfully. "Fancy comin' all this way to see that ole thing."

"GIVE THAT TO ME, BROWN," MR PERKINS SAID STERNLY.

"Come along, boys," called Mr Perkins fussily from the front, pushing William's bugle farther down into his pocket. "Don't dawdle there."

They straggled into the entrance hall, where the guide awaited them.

William listened without interest to an account of the various dates at which the various parts of the castle were built. The party straggled into the banqueting hall. A stream of dates and historical names again flowed unheeded past his ears while, in imagination, he faced an infuriated Robert. His eyes again wandered wistfully to the bugle that protruded from Mr Perkins's pocket. He wished he'd never touched the beastly thing. It was going to be the worst row he'd ever got into in all his life. The party followed the guide out of the banqueting hall towards the staircase. William straggled along at the end. At the foot of the staircase a small passage ran off at right angles and turned a corner. It looked rather an interesting little passage, and William felt a sudden desire to know what was round the corner. The other members of the Historical Society were surging ahead. No one was looking round. He slipped along the passage and turned the corner. Another little passage with a closed door at the end . . . Having satisfied his curiosity about the passage. William now felt an irresistible longing to satisfy his curiosity about the door. He approached it and listened. No sound came from within. The room – if room it was – must be empty. He'd just open it, peep in, then run back to join the Historical Society on their journey up the stone staircase. He opened it and peeped in. A small sunny sitting room, furnished in a refreshingly modern manner, as it seemed to William, who had just come from the banqueting hall . . . At first he did not see the old lady who sat in a bath chair by the window, wearing a shawl. He did not see her, in fact, till she said sharply:

"Well, come in, come in . . . Don't stand there like that."

William was so taken aback that he obeyed automatically.

"And you should knock at the door before you open it," went on the old lady severely.

William gaped at her, still too much taken aback to speak. The old lady glanced at the clock.

"And you're ten minutes late," she continued. "You were late yesterday, too. You must—" She looked at him and broke off. "A different boy again," she commented. "Dear, dear! I never knew anyone like you modern boys. Aren't you ever satisfied with a job? Why did the other boy go?"

"I don't know," said William truthfully.

"Well, come along. Don't waste any more time. Push

me out into the garden. I'm tired of telling a different gardener's boy every day what to do. I don't know whether it's the gardener's fault or yours that he can't keep a boy." She looked William up and down. "In your case it'll be yours, I expect. You don't look as if you could keep any job for more than a day. Well, hurry up. You've wasted half the morning already."

William hesitated. She seemed rather annoyed, and he felt that any explanation of the true state of the case would only annoy her still further. And, after all, wheeling the old lady round the garden would probably be as interesting as following the guide round the rotten old castle, with everyone jeering at him for having had his bugle confiscated.

"Push me out into the garden," went on the old lady, "and wheel me gently round the path. *Gently*, I said. What on earth does the boy think I am? Don't jerk the chair about like that. Smoothly and *gently* . . ."

It was a small, private-looking garden, enclosed by a yew hedge. William wheeled her round the path.

"What's your name?" said the old lady suddenly.

"William."

"That's better than some of them. The last was called Percival. His friends called him Perce. You're called Bill, I suppose?"

William gave a non-committal grunt.

"You're smaller than the others," went on the old lady. "You must be small for your age. Are you glad to have left school?"

William gave a gasp of envy. So the boy he was supposed to be had left school. Lucky beggar! Then slowly he became the boy who had left school and his face radiated triumphant freedom.

"Yes, I jolly well am," he said.

"Why?" said the old lady.

William began to expound his views on the general uselessness of education, the waste of time involved, the wear and tear of brain power, the continual interference with other and more useful pursuits.

"I can't think why someone hasn't stopped it years ago," he ended eloquently. "They stop slavery an' cruelty to animals an' suchlike an' yet they let a thing like school go on an' on an' on."

The old lady chuckled.

"Yes," she said, "I quite see your point of view. I used to feel just like that about it myself when I was your age. However, we've both left now so we can crow over people who haven't. By the way, there's a party of them coming round today. Generally my nephew doesn't let anyone come round while I'm staying with him, because I dislike people poking and prying about the place when I'm in it, but this boys' school wanted to come over, so he let them. Unlike you and me, he has a great respect for educational institutions. I wonder if they've arrived yet. Did you see them?"

"Yes," said William.

"Nasty little things. I hate boys. What did they look like?"

"The boys looked all right," said William. "I didn't like the look of the master, though."

"No, you wouldn't," said the old lady, "and I don't suppose he liked the look of you."

They had reached a garden seat and she raised her

hand imperiously. "Stop here. You may sit down on the seat. I've never been so badly wheeled before in my life. I'm almost bumped to death."

William sat down on the seat and stared in front of him, still lost in gloomy contemplation of the scenes that would take place when the loss of the bugle was discovered, thinking with ever increasing bitterness of Mr Perkins, who was even now wandering about the historic mansion with his ill-gotten booty sticking out of his coat pocket.

"Well, don't go to sleep," said the old lady sharply. "Tell me something more about yourself. What do you do when you aren't working? When you aren't supposed to be working, that is. I don't suppose you ever really work. What sort of games do you like playing?"

William tore himself from visions of vengeance to come, and began to describe the more exciting adventures that had recently befallen him – flights from irate landowners, pitched battles with rival gangs, Red Indian treks through the woods, then, throwing accuracy to the winds, went on to tell of his more imaginary exploits as a spy, as a Scotland Yard detective, as a Commander-in-Chief of the British Army.

The old lady chuckled again.

"I wish I'd know you sooner," she said. "I mean I wish I'd known you when I was a child. I think we'd have got on very well together. I used to have adventures just like that. I remember once I climbed to the top of the Great Pyramid and held thousands of Arabs at bay for three days till the rescuers arrived. Another time I boarded a pirate ship, alone and unarmed, locked them in the hold, and took the ship into the nearest harbour

"WHAT DO YOU DO WHEN YOU AREN'T WORKING?" ASKED THE OLD LADY.

and handed the pirates over to justice. There were about a hundred of them."

"I once did that too," said William, much interested.

"What are you going to be when you are grown up?"

"Well, I've not quite made up my mind whether to be a detective – a high-up detective, I mean – or a chimney sweep."

"I couldn't make up my mind whether to be a pirate or keep a sweet shop."

"Yes, both those are jolly good," agreed William. "I've thought of them, too."

At that moment they caught sight of a large figure in an opulent fur coat being shown into the little sitting room.

"Good Lord!" moaned the old lady. "It's Mrs Polkington. I can't face her. She stays for hours and talks about the 'Cause'."

"What Cause?" said William.

"The Cause of the moment. It's always a different one, but she always says just the same things about it. She's one of those women who have the energy of ten ordinary women – and no wonder, because they drain everyone they come across bone dry. She leaves me feeling like a piece of chewed string. I don't know why I'm telling you all this. I wouldn't have told any of the other boys. But I feel that we have a lot in common, and I tell you frankly that the thought of being talked to by that woman for the next two hours . . ."

"I'll stop her coming out to you," volunteered William.

"You can't. No one can."

"Let me try anyway."

"No, you couldn't possibly."

"I bet I could."

"You'd be rude to her or tell her lies, and I won't have that."

"No, I bet I can stop her without doin' either."

"Well, if you can, I'll give you anything you like. In reason, that is."

"All right," said William and set out towards the sitting room.

The lady in the fur coat had dismissed the housemaid with a wave of her hand ("I see where she is, my good girl. Don't trouble to announce me.") and was just stepping into the garden by the French window when she found William barring her way.

"She doesn't want to see you," he said.

His voice was low and respectful. He gazed at her sadly.

She stopped and stared at him.

"What do you mean?" she said haughtily.

He glanced at the figure of the old lady in the garden and lowered his voice confidentially.

"Well," he said, "I don't know if I ought to tell you."

"Do you mean that she's ill?" said Mrs Polkington. "If she's ill I must certainly go to her. She'll need me."

"Well," said William again in a mysterious voice, "I – well, I wouldn't go to her if I was you, that's all."

"But why not?" said Mrs Polkington, impressed, despite herself, by William's manner.

"She's – well, no one knows about it yet."

"Knows about *what*?"

"Of course it *may* not be that."

"May not be *what*?"

William sighed.

"Perhaps I oughtn't to have told you."

"You haven't told me anything," snapped the visitor.

William assumed a look of deep perplexity.

"I oughtn't to tell you," he said, "but – well, it isn't fair to let you go near her. Not till they know for certain. Of course if it isn't smallpox—" He clapped his hand to his mouth as if he had inadvertently let out a secret. "There now, I oughtn't to have told you."

"Smallpox!" said the lady, her eyes starting out of her head. "Good gracious! I always say that it's about a lot still, but people keep it dark. Smallpox! Fancy!"

"They don't know it's smallpox yet," said William hastily.

"What does the doctor say?"

"He's not been yet."

"I saw him at Gorse Villa as I came along. I suppose he's coming over here next. I thought he looked a bit worried. No wonder! Why on earth did that girl let me come into the house at all?"

"She doesn't know about it," said William.

"I suppose that's as well. You won't have a servant left in the house when they do. You're the gardener's boy, aren't you?"

"Uh-huh," said William.

"A new one again?"

"Uh-huh."

"There's a new gardener's boy every time I come here. I hope you'll work hard and try to keep the job. You'll be the first that has done, if you do. Well, I shouldn't go too near her if I were you. She's very wise to stay in the open air like that. Nothing like open air for carrying germs off. I'm a great believer in it myself. Give her my love and sympathy, won't you?"

"Yes," said William.

"Goodbye and remember – don't go too near her."

She went hastily out of the room and out by the side door, staying to shake from her coat any germs that might happen to be clinging there.

William returned slowly to the old lady.

"You don't mean to say she's gone?" said the old lady.

"Oh, yes, she's gone all right," William assured her.

"How did you do it?"

"Oh, I jus' did it," said William nonchalantly.

"Were you rude to her?"

"No."

"Did you tell her any lies?"

"No," said William, "I didn't say anything that wasn't true."

"Well, you're the only person who's ever managed to get rid of Lucy Polkington. Did she send a message?"

"Yes. She sent you her love an' sympathy."

"Sympathy. Why sympathy?"

"She jus' said that. She jus' said love an' sympathy."

"Well, she's gone – which is the main thing. I felt I couldn't have endured her today. There are certain people whom one can't endure on certain days. I'm very grateful to you, William. Let me see, I promised you anything you wanted, in reason, didn't I? What would you like?"

"A bugle," said William.

"A *what*?"

"A bugle."

"Why a bugle? I don't know anything about bugles. Don't you want anything but a bugle?"

"No, I'm afraid I don't," said William. "It doesn't matter if you've not got one, but it's the only thing I want jus' now."

"*Why* do you want a bugle?"

"Well, I can't quite explain," said William slowly. "It's sort of rather a long story. But it's jus' the only thing I want jus' now."

"You'll get the sack if you start on a bugle. One of them – it was either Perce or Syd, I've forgotten which – got it for a penny whistle. What about a nice pencil case?"

"No, thank you," said William politely.

"Or a nice penknife?"

"No, thank you," said William, still more politely.

The old lady sighed.

"Well, I've never seen anyone worst Lucy Polkington before in all my life, so let it be a bugle. But what *sort* of a bugle? I don't know anything about bugles. I expect there are hundreds of different kinds."

William was silent for some moments, then said:

"I saw jus' the sort I want today."

"Where?"

"That master that came with those boys had one sticking out of his coat pocket an' it was just the sort I want."

"How odd of him! What was he doing with a bugle sticking out of his pocket?"

"Well, he had one," said William, as if quite unable to explain the mystery, " 'cause I saw it."

"Perhaps he uses it to call them together or something. Schoolmasters are always rather odd."

"Yes, p'raps he uses it for that," agreed William.

"Look! They're coming here. What a nuisance! They've no right to come here. Oh, I remember, my nephew mentioned that he'd given them permission to come and look at the yew hedge. This wretched man who's brought them is keen on gardening, it seems. Here they are!"

"I think I'd better go an' – an' do a little weeding," said William, hastily diving out of sight behind a laurel bush. His voice came muffled by distance and the laurel bush. "Yes, there's a jolly lot of weeds here. I'll be some time in here gettin' them up."

After a moment or two Mr Perkins and his flock entered the garden.

"Now listen, boys, and stop scuffling," said Mr Perkins in his thin, high-pitched voice. "This is one of the most famous yew hedges in the country. Notice the—" He caught sight of the old lady and took off his hat with a flourish. "I beg your pardon, madam. I didn't notice that the garden was occupied. Perhaps . . ." He made a courteous gesture, as if to withdraw himself and his flock.

"Oh, no," she said, "it's quite all right. My nephew told me that he'd given you permission to show your boys this garden. Look round by all means. I don't like boys, but I realise that they're a necessary evil, which reminds me . . ." She glanced at Mr Perkins's pocket from which the mouth of the bugle boldly protruded. "Is that a bugle?"

Mr Perkins followed her gaze.

"Er – yes," he said, slightly embarrassed. "Yes, it is a – er – a bugle."

"May I look at it?" said the old lady.

Mr Perkins took it from his pocket with a flourish and handed it to her. She examined it curiously.

"And where can one buy such a thing?" she said.

"I – er – I'm afraid I really don't know," said Mr Perkins, still more embarrassed.

"That's rather unfortunate," said the old lady, "I thought that as you carried one about with you you'd probably know something about them."

"Well – er – I dare say I could find out," said Mr Perkins unhappily. "As a matter of fact—"

"Oh, never mind," interrupted the old lady. "Only I wanted to give one to a boy who'd done me a good turn." She glanced round for William. "The gardener's boy. He seems to be still weeding. He's a strange boy, but I promised him a bugle, and I haven't the faintest idea of how to set about getting one. When I found that you carried one about with you I thought that you might know."

"Well – er . . ." stammered Mr Perkins, then suddenly an idea occurred to him. He beamed ecstatically. He had been afraid that there'd be trouble about this bugle. It probably didn't really belong to that little wretch, and its owner would probably raise hell to get it back. The boy's father might even take a hand and come interfering and trying to bully him, as young Timpkins's father had done. Well, he'd stood his ground over that, and he'd stand his ground over this, whoever came interfering and trying to bully him. He'd never given back a confiscated article yet, and he wasn't going to start now. But the process of standing his ground was always rather wearing. Irate letters from irate fathers, irate visits from irate mothers, demanding back what they considered was their property. How much simpler it would be if he could just say that he'd given the thing away! No one could insist on its return then. It would take all the wind out of their sails. And it would be a very graceful act to give it to this dear old lady, who wanted it for some deserving boy – the sort of boy, apparently, who did people good turns and weeded gardens and that sort of thing – a very different type from that little wretch Brown. He glanced round. Unfortunately that little wretch Brown didn't seem to be here.

Dawdling about, he supposed, making a nuisance of himself somewhere or other, holding up the whole party when the time came for setting off home. He'd have liked him to be here to see his bugle given away. And he'd have liked the other boy to be here, too, so that that little wretch Brown could see a well-behaved boy – the very opposite of himself – being rewarded for his good behaviour. It might have been a useful object lesson.

He took the bugle from his pocket and handed it to the old lady with a courtly bow.

"I'd be most grateful, madam, if you would kindly accept this."

"Oh, but surely you need it, don't you?" said the old lady, taken aback.

"No, I don't," said Mr Perkins firmly. "I – er – I never really use it, and I'd be only too grateful to you if you would accept it."

"Well," said the old lady, taking it into her hand, "it's a cumbersome sort of thing to carry about with you if you never use it. It'll ruin the fit of your coat. You're *quite* sure you don't want it? It's exceedingly kind of you."

"Not at all," said Mr Perkins with another courtly bow.

"I'm sure the boy will be most grateful. He seemed set on a bugle."

"Please give it to him with my best wishes," said Mr Perkins, "and tell him from me that I'm glad that it should be given to someone who really deserves it."

After further exchanges of courtesies Mr Perkins conducted his flock out of the garden, and William emerged from the laurel bush.

"I'D BE MOST GRATEFUL, MADAM, IF YOU'D KINDLY ACCEPT THIS."

"Finished your weeding?" said the old lady.

"Yes, thanks," said William.

"What have you done with the weeds?" said the old lady, looking round. "Eaten them?"

"Yes," said William absently, then hastily correcting himself. "No."

"Well, here's your bugle. I suppose you heard what happened?"

"Er – yes. I did sort of hear," admitted William.

"Yes, I noticed you were weeding pretty quietly. Well, you're in luck. It looks quite a good article of its kind. What on earth was the man doing carrying it round with him if he doesn't use it? Still, it was kind of him to give it to me. Saved me a lot of trouble and expense. I can't think why I made a rash promise like that. After all, I don't suppose you've kept Lucy Polkington off for long. She'll be round again before evening. Listen . . . That's the charabanc come to take those boys away. Would you like to go and watch them set off? You can thank the man for giving you the bugle, too, if you like."

William made his way back to the front of the house where the boys were surrounding the charabanc. He held the bugle carefully hidden under his coat.

"Come along, Brown," snapped Mr Perkins. "Late as usual! What have you been doing all this time? We're just on the point of starting. Come along, come along, come along. And" – he continued on a note of triumph and self-satisfaction – "it's no use your asking me for that bugle back, because I've given it away. Given it away, you understand? Given it away."

Still smiling a smile of self-satisfaction and triumph (*that* would teach the little wretch) Mr Perkins climbed into the coach. William, too, climbed into the coach, still holding the bugle under his coat. The coach started off with its cargo of bored and weary boys. A short distance down the road they met a little crowd of people, headed by Mrs Polkington. It was the entire neighbourhood coming to see how the old lady's smallpox was. They had called at the doctor's and found him out. They all carried germicide in various forms in order to protect themselves from infection.

"We won't go into the house," they were saying. "We'll just ask at the door. Of course they may have taken her to an isolation hospital by now."

Mr Perkins, pleased by the quietness and decorum of the exhausted boys, turned and threw a quiet glance round the charabanc. Then the smile froze on his face. That Brown boy sat, quite quiet and well behaved – so quiet and well behaved that one could have no possible handle against him – holding a bugle on his lap. A *bugle. Another* bugle. How on earth had he got hold of another bugle. Or – *was* it another bugle? Mr Perkins's imagination fairly boggled. How could he have got hold of another bugle during the afternoon? And yet – how could it be the same? He'd given the original one to the old lady for her gardener's boy. This Brown boy couldn't, surely, have taken it from the gardener's boy. He was capable of anything. But, no, that was impossible. There wouldn't have been time. They'd set off almost as soon as he'd given it to the old lady. It was all most mysterious. *Most* mysterious. He fixed a stern gaze on William's face. William met the stern gaze so blandly and unflinchingly that Mr Perkins turned round to ruminate over the problem in silence. His mind went round and round in a circle. How could it be the same bugle? And yet, how could he have got hold of another? And yet, how could it be the same? His mind began to feel dizzy. He wondered whether to accost William and question him, but decided not to. There was something in that bland and unflinching stare that warned him not to. He was the sort of boy with whom it wasn't safe to interfere unless you were absolutely sure of your ground, and Mr Perkins wasn't absolutely sure of his ground. How could anyone be sure of his ground in the extraordinary circumstances?

"I thought the corbels in the banqueting hall were most interesting, didn't you, Mr Perkins?" said Blinks Major conversationally.

"Most interesting," agreed Mr Perkins absently, "yes – er – most interesting."

His mind was going round and round and round. How could it be the same bugle? And yet, how could it be another? And yet, how could it be the same? And yet, how could it be another? And yet, how could it be the same? He began to feel dizzier and dizzier.

"Smallpox?" the old lady was saying indignantly. "Who on *earth* said I'd got smallpox?"

"The boy," replied Mrs Polkington. "The boy who came to me in your sitting room."

"Oh, the gardener's boy."

"I suppose so."

"Did he say I'd got smallpox?"

"Well, actually," said Mrs Polkington, "he said that they didn't know whether it was smallpox yet, but naturally I—"

The old lady chuckled.

"I see." She looked round. "I gave him permission to go and see those schoolboys set off, and he's not come back yet. I expect he's got the sack by now, anyway. I told him he wouldn't keep the job a day. No, dear Lucy. I've not got smallpox. The boy, probably, misunderstood something I said. These boys *are* so stupid, you know. Oh, here's the gardener."

A rubicund, burly-looking man approached and touched his cap.

"I'm sorry the boy never turned up, your ladyship," he said.

"The new boy? Oh, he turned up all right, but I've not seen him for the last half-hour."

"Beg pardon, my lady, but he never come at all. I had a note from his mother to say that he'd broke his leg."

"But a boy *was* here."

"Beg pardon, my lady, no boy's been here today."

"But there was a boy here. I gave him a bugle."

"One of them schoolboys went off a-carryin' of a bugle," said the gardener. "An untidy-looking little varmint, he was."

"With his stockings coming down?"

"Yes."

"And his tie crooked?"

"Yes. I heard 'em call him William."

"William," said the old lady musingly. William . . . Smallpox . . . Bugle . . . A most mysterious affair. But, probably, quite simple if one knew the explanation. Mysterious things always were.

She chuckled again suddenly.

"Oh, well, we've all had a little excitement this afternoon. William, probably, most of all."

CHAPTER SIX

WILLIAM AND THE FISHERMAN

EVERY JUNE William's father went alone to a country inn for ten days' fishing. William had often begged to be allowed to accompany him, but his requests had always been met by such an uncompromising refusal that he had long since given up all hope. This year, however, to his surprise and delight Fate seemed to be on his side. He had had chicken-pox, and the doctor had decreed that a change of air was necessary before he returned to school.

His mother could not leave her housekeeping duties. The various relatives to whom (though without much real hope) she confided the problem replied kindly and sympathetically, but carefully refrained from inviting William to stay with them.

"You're going away next week, aren't you, dear?" said Mrs Brown to her husband innocently.

He looked at her suspiciously.

"If you mean will I take William," he said firmly, "I most decidedly will not."

But he felt much less firm on the point than he sounded.

If the doctor said that William must have a change of

air and he was the only member of the family going away, he didn't see how he could very well refuse to take him with him. He wrote to several relatives who had not yet been approached asking them bluntly if they would care to have William for a few days. They replied as bluntly that they would not.

"Mind you," said Mr Brown to his wife after having received the last of these replies, "if that boy comes with me, he must look after himself. I'm not going to be responsible for him in any way."

William, on learning that he was to go with his father on the fishing holiday that had been his Mecca from babyhood, could hardly contain his excitement.

He imagined himself accompanying his father and his friends upon all their fishing expeditions. He saw himself making huge catches of trout and salmon before admiring crowds of onlookers. His father seemed to be taking innumerable fishing rods with him, and William, ever an optimist, thought that he would probably lend him the ones he was not actually using. If his father happened to be using all his rods at once, William then would use his own fishing rod – a home-made implement consisting of a stick, a piece of string and a bent pin, with which he had distinguished himself at minnow-catching in all the local streams. If it would catch minnows, there was, William decided, no reason why it should not catch trout or even salmon . . . He set off with his father, full of hope, confidence, and excitement.

For the first day, he was busy assimilating his impressions. The inn – its clientele consisted entirely of angling enthusiasts – was full of large, purposeful-looking men to whom fishing was real, fishing was earnest; men who treated with silent contempt any remark that did not bear directly and intelligently upon the subject of fishing. At mealtimes they sat round a large table in the dining room in a grim silence broken only by such remarks as: "There was a good hatch of Mayfly about quarter past three", or "They were rising all right, but we couldn't find out what they were taking." Directly after breakfast they would garb themselves in all-enveloping diver-like costumes, collect their tackle and set off, still silent, grim, and purposeful, each to his favourite haunt.

They would not return till the evening and then it was the custom that each should silently and with modest pride lay his catch upon the marble-slabbed hatstand in the hall of the inn – each catch carefully separate and apart from the others. No one talked of his catch. He merely laid it upon the hatstand and waited for someone to ask whose it was. News of each catch spread quickly through the community. After dinner again the sportsmen sallied out, solemnly, purposefully, grimly, for the "night rise".

William watched all this with breathless interest. The thought of forming a part of such a community filled him with a fierce and burning pride.

On the first day his father asked him if he would like to come out with him in a boat, and William eagerly agreed. He found the day disappointing. His father landed him on an island in the lake with an empty tobacco box and instructions to catch Mayfly in the bushes. William caught three, then became bored and began to experiment with the damming of a small stream and finally to attempt the draining of a miniature bog into which he sank to his knees. When his father returned for him, the three Mayflies had escaped and his father, who immediately on reaching the fishing community had yielded to its pervading atmosphere of grim purposefulness, was coldly reproachful. The rest of the day was merely boring. The boatman would not let William try to row. His father would not let him try to fish. He got hopelessly entangled in a spare rod; he accidentally dropped overboard a box of flies that were unobtainable locally; he was bitten in the hand by a trout that he thought was dead, and thereupon gave a yell that put every other fish for miles around upon its guard.

He disgraced himself completely and finally by standing up to stretch away an attack of pins and needles, and overbalancing upon his father's rod and breaking it.

"I know one thing," said his father feelingly, "and that is that you're jolly well not coming out with me in the boat again."

William was not in any way perturbed by this sentence. It had been a boring and unsatisfactory day and he was convinced that a day spent by himself on dry land would be a much more enjoyable affair.

To his surprise and disgust, his father refused to lend him one of his rods. His father, it appeared, needed all his rods – either for "dapping" or "trolling" or "casting".

William considered that these people made far too complicated an affair of the simple exercise of fishing and set off alone with his home-made rod, a packet of sandwiches, and a basket lent to him for his "catch" by the landlady.

He found a suitable stream, fixed a worm on the bent pin at the end of his line, and began to fish. His luck was amazing. He caught minnow after minnow. He worked hard all morning and all afternoon and returned in the evening with a laden basket. The other fishermen had not yet returned. The marble top of the hatstand gleamed empty and inviting. William poured the contents of his basket upon it. They covered it completely with a shining heap of minnows. William gazed at them with fond pride. Then he got a piece of paper, wrote on it, "William Brown", and put it on top of the silvery heap. That done, glowing with triumph, he awaited the return of the other fishermen. Not one of them had ever completely filled the marble slab with a single catch like this. He had no doubt that he would be the hero of the evening.

Soon he heard the sound of someone approaching and stepped back modestly into the shadow. One of the fishermen – a stalwart young man with a projecting jaw and hooked nose – entered. He looked at the minnow-filled slab, scowled angrily, swept the whole gleaming heap on to the floor with an outraged gesture, rang the bell, said to the housemaid: "Clear up that mess," then with slow deliberate care placed a row of twelve trout on the slab.

William was speechless with indignation at the affront. His first impulse was to hurl himself savagely upon the young man; his second, based upon a consideration of the young man's powerful and muscular frame, was to contain his fury as best he could till an opportunity for a suitable revenge offered itself.

Up to now the fishermen had been identical in William's eyes. They were all large, single-purposed, unsmiling men dressed in enormous waders and devoid of any ideas outside the world of fishing.

Now each detached himself from the mass, as it were,

and assumed a distinct personality. There appeared to be two camps of them. The elder ones forgathered in the smoking room. William's father, who had come to the conclusion many years ago that William was quite capable of looking after himself, and who in any case had from the beginning announced his intention of not allowing him to interfere with his holiday, belonged to the elder camp, and in order to preserve the illusion of a Williamless holiday, had from the first forbidden William to enter the smoking room. So William, perforce, spent his time with the younger fishermen, and it was therefore the younger fishermen who he particularly studied.

The leader among them was the muscular youth addressed by his familiars as "Archie" who had swept William's magnificent catch so contemptuously on to the floor. Archie was the most skilful fisherman of the party. The others humbly asked his advice and appraised his prowess. Archie's row of trout on the hatstand slab was always longer than that of any of the others. Archie, moreover, knew the owner of a specially prolific reach of river, and had permission to fish there. He would return from his fishing expedition in this reach laden with spoils and more blatantly pleased with himself each time.

Archie was admired, his advice was sought on all sides, but not even his dearest friends could deny that Archie was overbearing and conceited. It soon became evident that he disliked William as much as William disliked him. The episode of the minnows seemed to him to be a deliberate affront to his dignity, and the presence of William among the party a perpetual outrage. He found fault with William continually, pushing him out of his way whenever he met him, with such lack of

THE FISHERMAN SCOWLED ANGRILY, AND SWEPT THE WHOLE HEAP ON TO THE FLOOR WITH AN OUTRAGED GESTURE.

ceremony that more than once he sent him sprawling to the ground. He made loud remarks in William's hearing on the unsuitability of having "kids mucking about the place".

"It's never happened before," he said, "and I hope to

WILLIAM WAS SPEECHLESS WITH INDIGNATION.

goodness that it'll never happen again. If it does I shall look out for another place."

William bided his time. He studied his enemy. There was no pretence about Archie's skill as a fisherman. William even followed him secretly down to his private post in the preserved reach and saw him catching trout after trout with an ease and ability that, despite his dislike, William could not help admiring.

He watched him standing in the swirling current in mid-stream up to his waist, still fishing with ease and ability. Certainly in his capacity as fisherman Archie was invulnerable. William tried to find some capacity in which he might be vulnerable, but could find none. For Archie seemed to be nothing but a fisherman. He seemed to have no instincts and desires but those of a fisherman. He seemed to function wholly and entirely upon the fishing plane.

The days passed swiftly by, and William, still enduring Archie's ceaseless snubs, almost began to give up hope of getting his own back. The last weekend of the holiday had arrived, and still Archie had revealed no weakness through which an enemy might avenge himself. His armour seemed to be jointless. Then – two days before William and his father were to return home – there arrived at the inn an elderly fisherman with his daughter.

The elderly fisherman was negligible enough, but the daughter was not. Even William could see at a glance that this was the sort of girl who made things hum. She had dimples, and dark, curling lashes shading eyes of the deepest blue. Her complexion was smooth and flawless. She had a shatteringly beautiful smile. And William, watching his enemy with ceaseless vigilance, realised at once that Archie was smitten, utterly and uncompromisingly smitten. Smitten, as the saying is, hip and thigh. Only the day before, Archie, after complaining for the thousandth time of having "kids messing about the place", had added: "But thank heaven, at least there aren't any women this year." But now William saw his tanned and healthy countenance deepen to a rich beetroot immediately his eyes fell upon this latest arrival.

The girl, whose name was Claribel, while apparently ignoring the youthful sportsmen and devoting herself entirely to her father, was obviously fully aware of the impression she had made. For not only Archie was smitten, but all the other members of the younger camp were smitten too.

It did not take long for the first shyness to wear off and then began the competition for the damsel's notice. And here Archie's friends, who should have rallied round him, basely deserted him. They did not sing his praises. They did not boost him to the skies as the world's best fisherman. They left him to sing his own praises and boost himself to the skies. To do him justice he was not backward. He boosted himself well and good. He enumerated his recent catches. He described how he alone of all the fishing party could fish with ease when up to his arms in a swirling torrent.

"It's partly a question of balance," he said, "and partly that I'm – well, I'm a fairly good fisherman, of course."

And Archie stroked his microscopic moustache complacently.

At first Claribel was amused, but gradually she became impressed.

"Come out in the boat with me tomorrow," said Archie, "I'm sure you'll enjoy it. I mean I'm sure you'll find it quite interesting."

Claribel agreed, and William saw yet another triumph in store for the hated Archie. For Claribel, he realised at once, despite her affection of hauteur, belonged to the class of "soppy girls". She swam with the stream and went with the crowd. If fishing were the fashion, then Claribel bags the best fisherman. And without doubt, Archie was the best fisherman. William was very thoughtful that evening.

"Who's the kid?' he heard Claribel ask of Archie.

And Archie replied contemptuously:

"A wretched little oik someone's brought with him."

The next morning was a perfect fishing morning, and Claribel, dressed very fetchingly in pale pink organdie, set off gaily to the river with Archie. He helped her into the boat with a courteous gesture, then the boatman pushed off.

"Isn't this jolly!" William heard Claribel say gaily. "Just like a picnic."

William unobtrusively followed the progress of the boat along the bank, slipping from bush to bush. The strident voice of Archie, enumerating his fishing exploits, reached him clearly across the water.

They reached a point in the river where, only the day before, Archie had stood in mid-stream, the water up to his armpits, "casting" with magnificent aplomb, and catching trout after enormous trout. He lowered himself from the boat and took up his stand, a smile of proud anticipation on his lips. He took up his stand and threw his line. Claribel watched him from the boat.

"Now start catching all those fishes you talk about," she said gaily.

Archie had cast his line stylishly enough, but the complacent expression on his face was giving way to uneasiness.

He smiled a ghastly smile at her and said: "Oh, yes . . .

you jolly well wait a few minutes . . ." Then the uneasiness of his expression deepened to panic.

"Hi!" he called suddenly, dropping his rod and clutching wildly at the air. "Hi! Help!"

The boatman hastily brought the boat up to him. He clutched frenziedly at the boatside and then at Claribel. He hung dripping round Claribel's neck. "I'm drowning!" he shouted. "Take me out quick!"

The boat rocked frantically. The boatman and Claribel between them dragged Archie into it. Claribel rendered this assistance involuntarily. Archie, having clasped his arms about her neck in his first spasm of terror, refused to unclasp them, and, long before his large and struggling body was safely landed in the boat, the pale pink organdie was a sodden mess, and Claribel was weeping with fury.

"I couldn't help it," panted Archie. "I t-tell you I was going under. I'd lost my balance. I'd have d-d-drowned if I hadn't caught hold of you. My waders were flooded. I can't th-th-think how. It's a miracle I wasn't drowned. I can't think *how* I wasn't drowned."

"I wish you had been," burst out Claribel passionately. "You've ruined my dress."

"Here's the hole, sir," said the boatman, pointing to an almost imperceptible slit just above the waist of Archie's waders.

"I can't think how it came there," said Archie. "They were all right yesterday." Then to Claribel: "I couldn't help it, I tell you."

"Of *course* you could help it," stormed Claribel. "Making a fool of yourself and me like that! *Deliberately* ruining everything I've got on. I'm soaked, and my dress is *ruined*, I tell you. Take me home at once. I shall never speak to you again as long as I live."

The boatman retrieved the rod, and rowed them back to the landing place, Archie protesting loudly, Claribel, who had had her say, now gazing over his head with an expression of icy contempt.

William did not come out of cover till they had vanished from view. Then he walked slowly homeward, tenderly fingering the penknife that had punctured Archie's waders and self-esteem.

But William never left anything to chance. He himself had an elder sister of great personal charm, and he had long studied with interest and perpetual surprise the way of a maid with a man. He had learnt that the more angry and unrelenting the maid seems at the actual moment of provocation, the sooner is she likely to relent. So that when he reached the inn he was not surprised to find Claribel and Archie on friendly terms again. Claribel had changed into a blue linen dress that was very becoming, so becoming in fact that she could not help feeling on good terms with herself and the whole world. She was even viewing the episode through a haze of glamour and looking on herself as having rescued Archie from a watery grave. Archie, with more sense than William would have given him credit for, was encouraging this view.

"I simply don't know what I'd have done if you hadn't happened to be there," he was saying.

"Well, of course," said Claribel modestly, "I always have been considered rather fearless. I mean, I do know how to keep my head in a crisis. I just saw what to do and did it. I'm like that."

"It was wonderful of you," said Archie fervently,

"simply *wonderful*. I believe that it's the first morning I've ever come in without catching a single fish. I'll go down to the river this afternoon, however, and see if I can make up for it."

"I expect you will if all I hear of your fishing is true," said Claribel sweetly.

It was very trying for William, after all the trouble he had taken, to see Archie resuming his old intolerable conceit and Claribel gradually softening towards him. But he had prepared for this, too. Not for nothing had he trudged yesterday into the nearest market town. Moreover, his knowledge of human nature served him well. He was sure that Claribel, after her morning's wetting, would not want to accompany Archie on his afternoon's fishing expedition.

So Archie set off alone. He was away for several hours, and when he returned he proudly laid twelve trout upon the hatstand, and went to summon Claribel to admire.

He did not see William slip into the hall as he went out of it. When he returned to it with Claribel he saw no difference in the fish that he had laid there. It was Claribel who discovered a wet and illegible fishmonger's ticket adhering to one of them. Claribel whose small but perfect nose discovered the distinctly unpleasant odour of the thirteenth fish – unlucky enough for Archie – that William had deftly introduced into the row. It was in vain that Archie protested and pleaded, in vain that he brought proof incontrovertible that he had actually caught the fish.

Claribel's anger of the afternoon had returned redoubled.

"A nasty, mean, low-down trick to play on me!" she fumed. "A cheat, that's what you are! A nasty, common cheat! Trying to make me think you'd caught them when you'd bought every *one* of them at a fishmonger's – and one of them bad at that! First you try to drown me – yes, and nearly *did* drown me. I could get you put in prison for attempted murder for this morning. I'm sure I could. It was a plot to *murder* me. I don't believe there was a hole in your waders. Or if there was you put it there. And then when you've not been able to murder me you try to make a fool of me by pretending to have caught fish when you've been out to buy them. I hate you, and I'll never speak to you again as long as I live. I always thought fishermen were cheats and liars, and now I know they are. *And* murderers. I hate all of you. I shan't stay a minute longer in the beastly place."

Leaving Archie opening and shutting his mouth silently like one of his own expiring fish, she swept into the smoking room, where her father was swapping fishing yarns with some members of the elder camp. He was surprised but in no way discomposed by his daughter's sudden decision to go home. He had long ago accustomed himself to sudden changes of plans on the part of his female belongings. Moreover, he knew that she had only accompanied him on an impulse, leaving behind her several interesting "affairs" from which a good deal of kick could still be extracted. He had had a suspicion that the place would fail to supply the excitement that was necessary to a girl of Claribel's temperament, and on the whole was not sorry to hear her decision.

"All right, my dear," he said mildly, "but I'm afraid

you can't leave this minute, because there isn't a train till tomorrow afternoon."

She did not come downstairs that evening. She spent it packing in her bedroom, while Archie hung about the hall, still opening and shutting his mouth silently, as if practising passionate speeches of protestation.

The next morning after breakfast Claribel directed the shattering smile at William and said: "Will you come for a walk with me this morning, William?"

William accepted the invitation with apparent eagerness, though he remained completely unshattered by the smile. He knew that Claribel had fixed on the "wretched little oik" with a true womanly intuition of what would be most galling to Archie. They spent the whole morning together. William found it intolerably boring. Claribel was the most limited human being whom he had ever met. She was wholly ignorant on the subject of pirates or smugglers or Red Indians. She was not interested in climbing trees, or damming streams, or getting through barbed-wire fences, or exploring the countryside. She was frightened of spiders, and she did not know a toad from a frog. Relations became definitely strained between them as the morning wore on, and Claribel grew more and more irritable, especially when William took her a short cut back to the inn that led directly through a bog. William persisted that the bog was now all right, as he had drained it three days before, but Claribel's dainty shoes bore ample evidence that this statement of William's erred on the side of optimism. Her resentment against the wretched Archie, however, still blazed so brightly that as soon as they came within sight of the inn she turned her shattering smile on to William again and began to talk to him with every appearance of affectionate interest.

The sight of Archie lurking morosely in the hall when they entered assured her that her efforts were not being wasted.

During lunch she continued to talk brightly to

"WILL YOU COME FOR A WALK WITH ME THIS MORNING, WILLIAM?" CLARIBEL ASKED.

William. After lunch the station bus drew up at the front door, and Claribel, attired for the journey, stepped into it. Archie sprang forward desperately.

"Listen!" he said. "Just listen! Just let me explain!"

But Claribel turned to William with the shattering smile and said:

"Goodbye, William darling, and thank you so much for being so sweet to me."

Then the bus swept her away, still waving effusively to William. Archie gave a hollow laugh, and William slipped away before Archie should try to find outlet for his feelings.

William and his father were going home the next day, so it was not difficult for William to avoid Archie's vengeance in the interval.

Failing to find William, Archie wreaked his vengeance on the fishes and brought in a phenomenal catch that he flung carelessly upon the slab, repeating the hollow laugh.

"Did you enjoy it, William dear?" asked William's mother when he reached home.

William considered the question in silence for a moment, then said:

"Yes, on the whole, I did – quite . . . especially the end part."

CHAPTER SEVEN

WILLIAM AND THE SMUGGLER

WILLIAM'S FAMILY were going to the seaside for February. It was not an ideal month for the seaside, but William's father's doctor had ordered him a complete rest and change.

"We shall have to take William with us, you know," his wife had said as they discussed plans.

"Good heavens!' groaned Mr Brown. "I thought it was to be a *rest* cure."

"Yes, but you know what he is," his wife urged. "I daren't leave him with anyone. Certainly not with Ethel. We shall have to take them both. Ethel will help with him."

Ethel was William's grown-up sister.

"All right," agreed her husband finally. "You can take all responsibility. I formally disown him from now till we get back. I don't care *what* trouble he lands you in. You know what he is and you deliberately take him away with me on a rest cure!"

"It can't be helped, dear," said his wife mildly.

William was thrilled by the news. It was several years since he had been at the seaside.

"Will I be able to go swimmin'?"

"It *won't* be too cold! Well, if I wrap up warm, will I be able to go swimmin'?"

"Can I catch fishes?"

"Are there lots of smugglers smugglin' there?"

"Well, I'm only *askin'*, you needn't get mad!"

One afternoon Mrs Brown missed her best silver tray and searched the house high and low for it wildly, while dark suspicions of each servant in turn arose in her usually unsuspicious breast.

It was finally discovered in the garden. William had dug a large hole in one of the garden beds. Into the bottom of this he had fitted the tray and had lined the sides with bricks. He had then filled it with water and taking off his shoes and stockings stepped up and down his narrow pool. He was distinctly aggrieved by Mrs Brown's reproaches.

"Well, I was practisin' paddlin', ready for goin' to the seaside. I didn't *mean* to rune your tray. You talk as if I *meant* to rune your tray. I was only practisin' paddlin'."

At last the day of departure arrived. William was instructed to put his things ready on his bed, and his mother would then come and pack for him. He summoned her proudly over the balusters after about twenty minutes.

"I've got everythin' ready, Mother."

Mrs Brown ascended to his room.

Upon his bed was a large pop-gun, a football, a dormouse in a cage, a punchball on a stand, a large box of "curios", and a buckskin which was his dearest possession and had been presented to him by an uncle from South Africa.

Mrs Brown sat down weakly on a chair.

"You can't possibly take any of these things," she said faintly but firmly.

"Well, you *said* put my things on the bed for you to pack an' I've put them on the bed, an' now you say—"

"I meant clothes."

"Oh, *clothes!*" scornfully. "I never thought of *clothes.*"

"Well, you can't take any of these things, anyway."

William hastily began to defend his collection of treasures.

"I *mus'* have the pop-gun 'cause you never know. There may be pirates an' smugglers down there, an' you can *kill* a man with a pop-gun if you get near enough and know the right place, an' I might need it. An' I *must* have the football to play on the sands with, an' the punchball to practise boxin' on, an' I *must* have the dormouse, 'cause – 'cause to feed him, and I *must* have this box of things and this skin to show to folks I meet down at the seaside 'cause they're int'restin'."

But Mrs Brown was firm, and William reluctantly yielded.

In a moment of weakness, finding that his trunk was only three-quarters filled by his things, she slipped in his beloved buckskin, while William himself put the pop-gun inside when no one was looking.

They had been unable to obtain a furnished house, so had to be content with a boarding house. Mr Brown was eloquent on the subject.

"If you're deliberately turning that child loose into a boarding house full, presumably, of quiet, inoffensive people, you deserve all you get. It's nothing to do with me. I'm going to have a rest cure. I've disowned him. He can do as he likes."

"It can't be helped, dear," said Mrs Brown mildly.

Mr Brown had engaged one of the huts on the beach chiefly for William's use, and William proudly furnished its floor with the buckskin.

"It was killed by my uncle," he announced to the small crowd of children at the door who had watched with interest his painstaking measuring on the floor in order to place his treasure in the exact centre. "He killed it dead – jus' like this."

William had never heard the story of the death of the buck, and therefore had invented one in which he had gradually come to confuse himself with his uncle in the rôle of hero.

"It was walkin' about an' I – he – met it. I hadn't got no gun, and it sprung at me an' I caught hold of its neck with one hand an' I broke off its horns with the other, an' I knocked it over. An' it got up an' ran at me – him – again, an' I jus' tripped it up with my foot an' it fell over again, an' then I jus' give it one big hit with my fist right on its head, an' it killed it an' it died!"

There was an incredulous gasp.

Then there came a clear, high voice from behind the crowd.

"Little boy, you are not telling the truth."

William looked up into a thin, spectacled face.

"I wasn't tellin' it to you," he remarked, wholly unabashed.

A little girl with dark curls took up the cudgels quite needlessly in William's defence.

"He's a very *brave* boy to do all that," she said indignantly. "So don't you go *saying* things to him."

"Well," said William, flattered but modest. "I didn't say I did, did I? I said my uncle – well, partly my uncle."

Mr Percival Jones looked down at him in righteous wrath.

"You're a very wicked little boy. I'll tell your father – er – I'll tell your sister."

For Ethel was approaching in the distance and Mr Percival Jones was in no way loath to converse with her.

Mr Percival Jones was a thin, pale, æsthetic would-be poet who lived and thrived on the admiration of the elderly ladies of his boarding house, and had done so for the past ten years. Once he had published a volume of poems at his own expense. He lived at the same boarding house as the Browns, and had seen Ethel in the distance at meals. He had admired the red lights in her dark hair and the blue of her eyes, and had even gone so far as to wonder whether she possessed the solid and enduring qualities which he would require of one whom in his mind he referred to as his "future spouse".

He began to walk down the beach with her.

"I should like to speak to you – er – about your brother, Miss Brown," he began, "if you could spare me the time, of course. I trust I do not – er – intrude or presume. He is a charming little man but – er – I fear – not veracious. May I accompany you a little on your way? I am – er – much attracted to your – er – family. I – er – should like to know you all better. I am – er – deeply attached to your – er – little brother, but grieved to find that he does not – er – adhere to the truth in his statements. I – er—"

"YOU'RE A VERY WICKED LITTLE BOY!" SAID MR PERCIVAL JONES.

Miss Brown's blue eyes were dancing with merriment.

"Oh, don't worry about William," she said. "He's *awful*. It's much best just to leave him alone. Isn't the sea gorgeous today?"

They walked along the sands.

Meanwhile William had invited his small defender into his hut.

"You can look round," he said graciously. "You've seen my skin what I – he – killed, haven't you? This is my gun. You put a cork in there and it comes out hard when you shoot it. It would kill anyone," impressively, "if you did it near enough to them and at the right place. An' I've got a dormouse, an' a punchball, an' a box of things, an' a football, but they wouldn't let me bring them," bitterly.

"It's a *lovely* skin," said the little girl. "What's your name?"

"William. What's yours?"

"Peggy."

"Well, let's be on a desert island, shall we? An' nothin' to eat nor anything, shall we? Come on."

She nodded eagerly.

"How *lovely!*"

They wandered out on to the promenade, and among a large crowd of passers-by bemoaned the lonely emptiness of the island and scanned the horizon for a sail. In the far distance on the cliffs could be seen the figures of Mr Percival Jones and William's sister, walking slowly away from the town.

At last they turned towards the hut.

"We must find somethin' to eat," said William firmly. "We can't let ourselves starve to death."

"Shrimps?" suggested Peggy cheerfully.

"We haven't got nets," said William. "We couldn't save them from the wreck."

"Periwinkles?"

"There aren't any on this island. I know! Seaweed! An' we'll cook it."

"Oh, how *lovely!*"

He gathered up a handful of seaweed and they entered the hut, leaving a white handkerchief tied on to the door to attract the attention of any passing ship. The hut was provided with a gas ring and William, disregarding his family's express injunction, lit this and put on a saucepan filled with water and seaweed.

"We'll pretend it's a wood fire," he said. "We couldn't make a real wood fire out on the prom. They'd stop us. So we'll pretend this is. An' we'll pretend we saved a saucepan from the wreck."

After a few minutes he took off the pan and drew out a long green strand.

"You eat it first," he said politely.

The smell of it was not pleasant. Peggy drew back.

"Oh, no, you first!"

"No, you," said William nobly. "You look hungrier than me."

She bit off a piece, chewed it, shut her eyes and swallowed.

"Now you," she said with a shade of vindictiveness in her voice. "You're not going to not have any."

William took a mouthful and shivered.

"I think it's gone bad," he said critically.

Peggy's rosy face had paled.

"I'm going home," she said suddenly.

"You can't go home on a desert island," said William severely.

"Well, I'm going to be rescued then," she said.

"I think I am, too," said William.

It was lunch time when William arrived at the boarding house. Mr Percival Jones had moved his place so as to be nearer Ethel. He was now convinced that she was possessed of every virtue his future "spouse" could need. He conversed brightly and incessantly during the meal. Mr Brown grew restive.

"The man will drive me mad!" he said afterwards. "Bleating away! What's he bleating about anyway? Can't you stop him bleating, Ethel? You seem to have influence. Bleat! Bleat! Bleat! Good Lord! And me here for a *rest* cure."

At this point he was summoned to the telephone and returned distraught.

"It's an unknown female," he said. "She says that a boy of the name of William from this boarding house has made her little girl sick by forcing her to eat seaweed. She says it's brutal. Does anyone *know* I'm here for a rest cure? Where is the boy? Good heavens! Where is the boy?"

But William, like Peggy, had retired from the world for a space. He returned later on in the afternoon, looking pale and chastened. He bore the reproaches of his family in stately silence.

Mr Percival Jones was in great evidence in the drawing room.

"And soon – er – soon the – er – Spring will be with us once more," he was saying in his high-pitched voice as he leant back in his chair and joined the tips of his fingers together. "The Spring – ah – the Spring! I have a – er – little effort I – er – composed on – er – the Coming of Spring – I – er – will read to you some time if you will – ah – be kind enough to – er – criticise – ah – impartially."

"*Criticise!*" they chorused. "It will be above criticism. Oh, do read it to us, Mr Jones."

"I will – er – this evening." His eyes wandered to the

door, hoping and longing for his beloved's entrance. But Ethel was with her father at a matinée at the Winter Gardens and he looked and longed in vain. In spite of this, however, the springs of his eloquence did not run dry, and he held forth ceaselessly to his little circle of admirers.

"The simple – ah – pleasures of nature. How few of us – alas! – have the – er – gift of appreciating them rightly. This – er – little seaside hamlet with its – er – sea, its – er – promenade, its – er – Winter Gardens! How beautiful it is! How few appreciate it rightly!"

Here William entered and Mr Percival Jones broke off abruptly. He disliked William.

"Ah! Here comes our little friend. He looks pale. Remorse, my young friend? Ah, beware of untruthfulness. Beware of the beginnings of a life of lies and deception." He laid a hand on William's head and cold shivers ran down William's spine. " 'Be good, sweet child, and let who will be clever,' as the poet says." There was murder in William's heart.

At that minute Ethel entered.

"No," she snapped. "I sat next to a man who smelt of bad tobacco. I *hate* men who smoke bad tobacco."

Mr Jones assumed an expression of intense piety.

"I may boast," he said sanctimoniously, "that I have never thus soiled my lips with drink or smoke . . ."

There was an approving murmur from the occupants of the drawing room.

William had met his father in the passage outside the drawing room. Mr Brown was wearing a hunted expression.

"Can I go into the drawing room?" he said bitterly, "or is he bleating away in there?"

They listened. From the drawing room came the sound of a high-pitched voice.

Mr Brown groaned.

"Good Lord!" he moaned. "And I'm here for a *rest* cure and he comes bleating into every room in the house. Is the smoking room safe? Does he smoke?"

Mr Percival Jones was feeling slightly troubled in his usually peaceful conscience. He could honestly say that he had never smoked. He could honestly say that he had never drunk. But in his bedroom reposed two bottles of brandy, purchased at the advice of his aunt "in case of emergencies". In his bedroom also was a box of cigars that he had bought for a cousin's birthday gift, but which his conscience had finally forbidden to present. He decided to consign these two emblems of vice to the waves that very evening.

Meanwhile William had returned to the hut and was composing a tale of smugglers by the light of a candle. He was much intrigued by his subject. He wrote fast in an illegible hand in great sloping lines, his brows frowning, his tongue protruding from his mouth as it always did in moments of mental strain.

His sympathies wavered between the smugglers and the representatives of law and order. His orthography was the despair of his teachers.

" *'Ho!' sez Dick Savage,"* he wrote. " *'Ho! Gadzooks! Rol in the bottles of beer up the beech. Fill your pockets with the baccy from the bote. Quick, now! Gadzooks! Methinks we are observed!' He glared round in the darkness. In less time than wot it takes to rite this he was srounded by pleesemen and stood, proud and defiant, in the light of there electrick torches wot they had wiped quick as litening from their busums.*

" 'Surrender!' cried one, holding a gun at his brain and a drorn sord at his hart, 'Surrender or die!'

" 'Never,' said Dick Savage, throwing back his head, proud and defiant. 'Never. Do to me wot you will I die.'

"One crule brute hit him a blo on the lips and he sprang back, snarling with rage. In less time than wot it takes to rite this he had sprang at his torturer's throte and his teeth met in one mighty bite. His torturer dropped dead and lifless at his feet.

" 'Ho!' cried Dick Savage, throwing back his head, proud and defiant, again, 'So dies any of you wot insults my proud manhood. I will meet my teeth in your throtes.'

"For a minit they stood trembling, then one, bolder than the rest, lept forward and tide Dick Savage's hands with rope behind his back. Another took from his pockets bottles of beer and tobacco in large quantities.

" 'Ho!' they cried exulting. 'Ho! Dick Savage the smuggler caught at last!'

"Dick Savage gave one proud and defiant laugh, and, bringing his tide hands over his head he bit the rope with one mighty bite.

" 'Ho! ho!' he cried, throwing back his proud head, 'Ho, ho! You dirty dogs!'

"Then, draining to the dregs a large bottle of poison he had concealed in his bosum he fell ded and lifless at there feet."

*

There was a timid knock at the door and William, scowling impatiently, rose to open it.

"What d'you want?" he said curtly.

A little voice answered from the dusk.

"It's me – Peggy. I've come to see how you are, William. They don't know I've come. I was awful sick after that seaweed this morning, William."

William looked at her with a superior frown.

"Go away," he said. "I'm busy."

"What are you doing?" she said, poking her little curly head into the doorway.

"I'm writin' a tale."

She clasped her hands.

"Oh, how lovely! Oh, William, do read it to me. I'd *love* it!"

Mollified, he opened the door and she took her seat on his buckskin on the floor, and William sat by the candle, clearing his throat for a minute before he began. During the reading she never took her eyes off him. At the end she drew a deep breath.

"Oh, William, it's beautiful. William, are there smugglers now?"

"Oh, yes. Millions," he said carelessly.

"*Here?*"

"Of course there are!"

She went to the door and looked out at the dusk.

"I'd love to see one. What do they smuggle, William?"

He came and joined her at the door, walking with a slight swagger as became a man of literary fame.

"Oh, beer an' cigars an' things. *Millions* of them."

A furtive figure was passing the door, casting suspicious glances to left and right. He held his coat tightly around him, clasping something inside it.

"I expect that's one," said William casually.

They watched the figure out of sight.

Suddenly William's eyes shone.

"Let's stalk him an' catch him," he said excitedly. "Come on. Let's take some weapons." He seized his pop-gun from a corner. "You take" – he looked round the room – "you take the waste-paper basket to put over his head an' – an' pin down his arms an' somethin' to tie him up! – I know – the skin I – he – shot in Africa. You can tie its paws in front of him. Come on! Let's catch him smugglin'."

He stepped out boldly into the dusk with his pop-gun, followed by the blindly obedient Peggy carrying the waste-paper basket in one hand and the skin in the other.

Mr Percival Jones was making quite a little ceremony of consigning his brandy and cigars to the waves. He had composed "a little effort" upon it which began:

"O deeps, receive these objects vile
Which nevermore mine eyes shall soil."

He went down to the edge of the sea and, taking a bottle in each hand, held them out at arms' length, while he began in his high-pitched voice:

"O deeps, receive these—"

He stopped. A small boy stood beside him holding out at him the point of what in the semi-darkness Mr Jones took to be loaded rifle. William mistook his action in holding out the bottles.

"It's no good tryin' to drink it up," he said severely. "We've caught you smugglin'."

Mr Percival Jones laughed nervously.

"My little man!" he said. "That's a very dangerous – er – thing for you to have! Suppose you hand it over to me, now, like a good little chap."

William recognised the voice.

"Fancy you bein' a smuggler all the time!" he said with righteous indignation in his voice.

"Take away that – er – nasty gun, little boy," pleaded his captive plaintively. "You – ah – don't understand it. It – er – might go off."

William was not a boy to indulge in half measures. He meant to carry the matter off with a high hand.

"I'll shoot you dead," he said dramatically, "if you don't do jus' what I tell you."

Mr Percival Jones wiped the perspiration from his brow.

"Where did you get that rifle, little boy?" he asked in a voice he strove to make playful. "Is it – ah – is it loaded? It's – ah – unwise, little boy. Most unwise. Er – give it to me to – er – take care of. It – er – might go off, you know."

William moved the muzzle of his weapon, and Mr Percival Jones shuddered from head to foot. William was a brave boy, but he had experienced a moment of cold terror when first he had approached his captive. The first note of the quavering high-pitched voice had, however, reassured him. He instantly knew himself to be the better man. His captive's obvious terror of his pop-gun almost

"WE'VE CAUGHT YOU SMUGGLING!" WILLIAM SAID SEVERELY.

persuaded him that he held in his hand some formidable death-dealing instrument. As a matter of fact Mr Percival Jones was temperamentally an abject coward.

"You walk up to the seats," commanded William. "I've took you prisoner for smugglin' an' – an' – jus' walk up to the seats."

Mr Percival Jones obeyed with alacrity.

"Don't – er – *press* anything, little boy," he pleaded as he went. "It – ah – might go off by accident. You might do – ah – untold damage."

Peggy, armed with the waste-paper basket and the skin, followed open-mouthed.

At the seat William paused.

"Peggy, you put the basket over his head an' pin his arms down – case he struggles, an' tie the skin wot I shot round him, case he struggles."

Peggy stood upon the seat and obeyed. Their victim made no protest. He seemed to himself to be in some horrible dream. The only thing of which he was conscious was the dimly descried weapon that William held out at him in the darkness. He was hardly aware of the waste-paper basket thrust over his head. He watched William anxiously through the basket-work.

"Be careful," he murmured. "Be careful, boy!"

He hardly felt the skin which was fastened tightly round his unresisting form by Peggy, the tail tied to one front paw. Unconsciously he still clasped a bottle of brandy in each arm.

Then came the irate summons of Peggy's nurse through the dusk.

"Oh, William," she said panting with excitement. "I don't want to leave you. Oh, William, he might *kill* you!"

"You go on. I'm all right," he said with conscious valour. "He can't do nothin' 'cause I've got a gun an' I can shoot him dead" – Mr Percival Jones shuddered afresh – "an' he's all tied up an' I've took him prisoner an' I'm goin' to take him home."

"Oh, William, you *are* brave!" she whispered in the darkness as she flitted away to her nurse.

William blushed with pride and embarrassment.

Mr Percival Jones was convinced that he had to deal with a youthful lunatic, armed with a dangerous weapon, and was anxious only to humour him till the time of danger was over and he could be placed under proper restraint.

Unconscious of his peculiar appearance, he walked before his captor, casting propitiatory glances behind him.

"It's all right, little boy," he said soothingly, "quite all right. I'm – er – your friend. Don't – ah – get annoyed, little boy. Don't – ah – get annoyed. Won't you put your – gun down, little man? Won't you let me carry it for you?"

William walked behind, still pointing his pop-gun.

"I've took you prisoner for smugglin'," he repeated doggedly. "I'm takin' you home. You're my prisoner. I've took you."

They met no one on the road, though Mr Percival Jones threw longing glances around, ready to appeal to any passer-by for rescue. He was afraid to raise his voice in case it should rouse his youthful captor to murder. He saw with joy the gate of his boarding house and hastened up the walk and up the stairs. The drawing room door was open. There was help and assistance, there was protection against this strange persecution. He entered, followed closely by William. It was about the time he had promised to read his "little effort" on the Coming of Spring to his circle of admirers. A group of elderly ladies sat round the fire awaiting him. Ethel was writing. They turned as he entered and a gasp of horror and incredulous dismay went up. It was that gasp that called him to a realisation of the fact that he was wearing a waste-paper basket over his head and shoulders, and that a mangy fur was tied round his arms.

"Mr *Jones*!" they gasped.

He gave a wrench to his shoulders and the rug fell to the floor, revealing a bottle of brandy clasped in either arm.

"Mr *Jones*!" they repeated.

"I caught him smugglin'," said William proudly. "I caught him smugglin' beer by the sea an' he was drinking those two bottles he'd smuggled an' he had thousands an' *thousands* of cigars all over him, an' I caught him, an' he's a smuggler, an' I brought him up here with my gun. He's a smuggler an' I took him prisoner."

Mr Jones, red and angry, his hair awry, glared through the wickerwork of his basket. He moistened his lips. "This is an outrage," he spluttered.

Horrified elderly eyes stared at the incriminating bottles.

"He was drinkin' 'em by the sea," said William.

"Mr *Jones*!" they chorused again.

"I CAUGHT HIM SMUGGLING," WILLIAM EXPLAINED PROUDLY. "HE HAD THOUSANDS AN' THOUSANDS OF CIGARS AND THAT BEER!"

He flung off his waste-paper basket and turned upon the proprietress of the establishment who stood by the door.

"I will not brook such treatment," he stammered in fury. "I leave your roof tonight. I am outraged – humiliated. I – I disdain to explain. I – leave your roof tonight."

"Mr *Jones*!" they said once more.

Mr Jones, still clasping his bottles, withdrew, pausing to glare at William on his way.

"You *wicked* boy! You *wicked* little, *untruthful* boy," he said.

William looked after him. "He's my prisoner an' they've let him go," he said aggrievedly.

Ten minutes later he wandered into the smoking room. Mr Brown sat miserably in a chair by a dying fire beneath a poor light.

"Is he still bleating there?" he said. "Is this still the only corner where I can be sure of keeping my sanity? Is he reading his beastly poetry upstairs? Is he—"

"He's goin'," said William moodily. "He's goin' before dinner. They've sent for his cab. He's mad 'cause I said he was a smuggler. He was a smuggler 'cause I saw him doin' it, an' I took him prisoner an' he got mad an' he's goin'. An' they're mad at me 'cause I took him prisoner. You'd think they'd be glad at me catchin' smugglers, but they're not," bitterly. "An' Mother says she'll tell you an' you'll be mad too an'—"

Mr Brown raised his hand.

"One minute, my son," he said. "Your story is confused. Do I understand that Mr Jones is going and that you are the cause of his departure?"

"Yes, 'cause he got mad 'cause I said he was a

smuggler an' he was a smuggler an' they're mad at me now, an'—"

Mr Brown laid a hand on his son's shoulder.

"There are moments, William," he said, "when I feel almost affectionate towards you."

CHAPTER EIGHT

WILLIAM AND THE SPY

THE MEMBERS of William's family were having their annual holiday by the sea. They were staying in the boarding house in which they generally stayed. The Browns chose it because it did not object to William. It was not enough for the Browns to go to a boarding house that did not object to children. It had to be one that did not object to William. This boarding house was of a philosophical, if pessimistic nature and took it as in the natural course of things that William's crabs should make their home in the hatstand drawer, that "pieces" from William's collection of seaweed should make the hall into a sort of skating rink, and that William himself should leave a trail of sand and shells and jellyfish wherever he went. William, however, was enjoying this holiday less than the other members of his family. Though indulging to the full in the delights of the seaside, he considered them to be greatly overrated. Paddling was a pastime whose possibilities were soon exhausted. He could make it exciting by pretending that he was wading into the sea to rescue shipwrecked sailors or pull to shore a boat of smuggled goods, but he always entered too whole-heartedly into these games and arrived home soaked to the neck. Paddling was generally forbidden by his mother after the third day at the seaside, because, as she said, he only had three suits, and, when he got them all soaked in one day, there was nothing to fall back on.

It happened to be too cold for swimming, for which Mrs Brown was thankful, because last year the other swimmers had grown so tired of rescuing William that they had threatened to let him drown the next time he got into difficulties.

When paddling was forbidden, William took to exploring the rocks with results even more disastrous than those of paddling, for there were pools of water among the rocks into which he was always falling, as well as jagged surfaces down which he was always sliding. His mother's attitude to this annoyed William almost beyond expression.

"How d'you think I'm ever goin' to be able to have any sort of adventure when I grow up if I don't try 'n' get a bit of practice now?" he protested passionately. "How d'you think Hereward the Wake'd ever have been a hero if his mother had gone on at him like what you do at me whenever he got his suits wet?"

"I don't know how many suits Hereward the Wake had," said Mrs Brown firmly, "but, if he only had three and had soaked two and torn the third, I don't see what his mother could have done but make him stay indoors till one of them was fit to wear."

And so it came about that William was sitting in the drawing room of the boarding house in his dressing gown, while two of his suits dried before the kitchen fire, and the third was at the tailor's having a new seat put in.

William had never patronised the drawing room

before, and the novelty of the situation rather intrigued him. There was an old lady in an armchair by the fire who had already requisitioned him to hold her wool for her to wind. William disliked holding wool for people to wind, and with a skill born of long practice had managed to get it into such a tangle without apparently moving his hands at all, that the old lady had given up the whole thing in despair and gone to sleep. On the other side of the fire sat another lady, tall and thin and middle-aged, engaged upon a piece of crochet work and wearing a pair of pince-nez balanced on the very end of her nose. Between her and the sleeping old lady was a circle of other ladies, all middle-aged and thin and spectacled and engaged upon needlework of some sort. William, clad in his dressing gown and forming part of the circle though completely ignored by it, gazed around at them with deep interest. He had had no idea that all these women were different. He always came in to meals when everyone else had finished, and, meeting these visitors occasionally in the passages, he had thought that there was only one of them.

Now he looked round at them with the thrill of the discoverer . . . One, two, three, four, five, six, and so much alike that he had thought they were all the same.

The one by the fire was talking. Her name was Miss Smithers. She had lived an utterly uneventful life and had never had anything to talk about till the war came. She hadn't yet realised that most people had stopped talking about the war.

"Of course," she was saying, "the country had been *full* of their spies for *years* before the war began. They'd come over as tourists or students or even professors –

and they'd pass as Englishmen *anywhere*, you know, they're such clever linguists – and they'd each take a tiny bit of the coastline and *study* it till they knew every *inch* of it. *Riddled* with spies, the country was. And what they've done once they can do again . . . We're never on our guard."

The others, who had heard it all before, were not taking any notice, but William was sitting forward, eyes and mouth wide open, drinking in her words. The war had been over before William was born, and William's immediate circle was one that lived in the present. He had never heard anything like this before . . . Most thrilling of all was the "And what they've done once they can do again."

He was just going to demand further details, when his mother opened the door to tell him one of his suits was dry now and he could go and put it on. He followed her into the hall. There stood an elderly man with a short, white beard talking to the proprietress. He held a suitcase in his hand and had evidently just arrived. He was saying, "I'm a geologist, you know. I've come here to study this part of the coast."

And then, of course, William knew beyond a shadow of doubt that he was a German spy who had come over to prepare for the next war.

"What's a geologist?" William asked his mother as he struggled into his suit that, though dry, was still strongly perfumed with seaweed.

"A man who studies rocks," said his mother.

William uttered an ironic laugh.

"That's a *jolly* easy way to do it," he said.

"What are you talking about?" said his mother, who was looking doubtfully at his suit and wondering whether it had been as much too small for him as that before its immersion in sea water.

But William merely repeated his ironic laugh.

The next morning William set off to a withdrawn spot among the rocks that had already served him as a Red Indian camp and a pirate's ship, and there he held a meeting of the secret service men under his command. They all saluted him respectfully as he entered – a magnificent figure in a blazing uniform with jingling spurs. He informed them curtly of the danger (there were, of course, innumerable Germans studying each a mile or so of the coast) and warned them that the work on which he was sending them would probably mean death (he was a ruthless man with no compunction at all in sending his men to their death, but he went to his own so bravely and so continually that they could not resent it). Then, after ordering them each to dog one spy and report to him daily, he gave them the secret code and password, and explained the complicated system of signals by which they were to communicate with each other and with him. He warned them to expect no mercy from him if they failed. That, of course, was part of his ruthlessness, for which nevertheless they all adored him. An ordinary passer-by would have seen nothing of this. He would merely have seen a small boy in a suit that had obviously suffered as the result of frequent immersion in sea water, playing by himself in a hollow among the rocks. Ordinary passers-by, of course, never see things as they really are.

At the end of the meeting William changed his rôle to that of one of the secret service men (the best and most promising of them, whose courage had already been tried in many a desperate adventure) and, saluting the magnificent figure in the resplendent uniform, emerged from the rocks after making elaborate precautions to escape detection. With his collar turned up, and his head sunk into it so deeply that nothing of his face could be seen but the tip of his nose, he set off in order to shadow his victim.

Professor Sommerton was not at all surprised to find himself dogged throughout the morning by a small boy. He had learnt that, wherever one was and whatever one was doing, small boys always hung about to watch and if possible annoy one. This small boy was rather odd in his behaviour (for instance one could see nothing at all of his face, as he kept his cap pulled down and his coat collar turned up, and he followed one in an extraordinary fashion, sidling along by the rocks), but then the professor considered all small boys to be odd in their behaviour, differing only in degrees of oddness, and he disliked them all uniformly. This boy, however, really began to get on his nerves as the morning wore on, and he returned to the boarding house earlier than he had meant to, only to discover to his annoyance that he had lost the sheet of paper on which he had been making his shorthand notes. At that very moment William was entering the hollow in the rocks still with elaborate precaution of secrecy – gazing round on all sides to see that the coast was clear and then pulling up his coat collar so high that one of the sleeves gave audibly beneath the strain – and handing the sheet of paper to the chief in the magnificent uniform.

"Here's his code what I've got at deadly peril," he was saying. "If he'd seen me he'd've killed me. He'd gotter special pistol in his pocket made to look like a fountain pen an' I bet if he'd've seen me I'd've been dead by now."

The magnificent chief read the paper with many a low whistle and exclamation of "Gosh!"

He said that none of the others had done so well and promoted William to be second-in-command.

"When you hear of me bein' killed by crim'nals," he said, "what I'm likely to be any minute, you jus' carry on here. Seems to me you're the bravest man I've ever come across – next to me, of course."

William went home well satisfied by his morning's work. The professor was less satisfied.

"Most tiresome," William heard him say at lunch. "I lost the paper on which were the results of my whole morning's work."

He met William's eye – a completely blank eye – and sighed. He did not connect William with the boy who had haunted him all the morning, but he felt vaguely that the world would be a more peaceful place if there were no small boys in it.

After lunch he went out to the rocks and set to work again. He had a tape measure and a little hammer, and he worked hard, stopping every now and then to make notes or to add to the contours of a rough map that he was making. Again the boy was there, peering at him between the buttonholes of his coat (which was pulled up till the collar was on a level with the top of his head, and which now showed a large rent round the sleeve), crawling after him on hands and knees, watching him from inadequate hiding places among the rocks, sidling around him in a way that distracted the professor indescribably. And then when he reached the boarding house he found that he had lost the map that contained the results of his afternoon's work.

William was seated in the hollow among the rocks. He had grown tired of the magnificent chief and had had him killed by criminals. He was holding a meeting of the other secret service men and telling them that the chief had been killed by criminals and that he was now in sole charge. He told them that he had got both the code and the map from his spy, and asked how they had been getting on. They had, of course, no results at all to show him, and he was very stern with them.

The professor set out the next morning with a firm determination to send that boy about his business – by force if needs be. The whole situation was getting on his nerves. He was sure that he would never have lost those papers if it hadn't been for that boy's distracting his attention by his antics.

He went a longer way down the coast than usual. William followed him as before, slipping from rock to rock. William was blissfully unaware that his quarry had even caught a glimpse of him. He imagined that, thanks to his methods of secrecy, he had been completely invisible to him all the time. It was therefore an unpleasant surprise when, as he was engaged on watching his victim on hands and knees from the shadow of a rock, his victim turned on him savagely and said:

"I've had enough of your monkey tricks, my boy. Clear off and be quick about it."

William rose to his feet with dignity. He thought it best now to reveal himself in his true colours.

"Yes," he said, "I bet you'd like me to clear off. I bet you don't know who I am?"

"Who are you then?" said the professor irritably.

"I know all about *you*," said William darkly. "I know what you're doin' an' where you've come from an' I've got your code so it's no use tryin' to send any secret messages, an' my men are all surroundin' you so it's no use trying to escape an'—"

"Clear off," roared the professor angrily, "and don't give me any more of your impudence."

William was slightly nonplussed by this attitude. The man should have been cowering at his feet and begging for mercy by now. Suddenly the professor made a threatening gesture with his hammer and roared again, "Clear off." William lost no time in clearing off. He told himself when he reached the promenade that his life was of too great service to his country for him to risk it unduly. He stood on the promenade wondering what to do. His afternoon's dogging of his victim had not improved his never-very-spruce appearance. His grown-up sister passed him at that moment with an immaculate youth in tow. She passed him with bated breath and eyes staring glassily in front of her, in fear lest William should see and recognise her. William was too much engrossed in his problem to have eyes for Ethel and her escort. In any case he cherished a healthy contempt for Ethel's idea of pleasure. He went down to the beach and threw stones idly into the sea while he pondered what was best to do. Some

"CLEAR OFF," ROARED THE PROFESSOR ANGRILY, "AND DON'T GIVE ME ANY MORE OF YOUR IMPUDENCE."

people who were swimming came out of the sea to remonstrate, and William moved away with dignity to an unattended boat, in which he sat trying to look as if it belonged to him and continuing his mental wrestling with his problems.

He might, of course, go to the hollow in the rocks to report, but he was growing tired of the hollow in the rocks. He had that morning, as he dressed, sent a messenger to dismiss all the other secret service workers so that he needn't be bothered with them any more. There was no doubt at all, however, that the man was a spy and that it was his duty to bring him to justice. He sat up and looked about him. Along the promenade a policeman was coming with slow and measured tread. That was the best thing to do, of course. Tell a policeman about it and leave him to catch the spy and put him in prison. William realised suddenly that there were a lot of interesting things he wanted to do, and that it would be quite a relief to get rid of his spy by handing him over to justice. He made his way up to the promenade and followed the policeman, dodging in and out of people's legs till he caught him up.

"Please!" he said breathlessly.

The policeman turned. He had a fierce moustache, and eyebrows that were fiercer still. William looked at him and decided to find one who looked a little more sympathetic before he told his tale.

"Well," the policeman had snapped, "what d'you want?"

"What's the time please?" said William meekly.

"Use your eyes," said the policeman, pointing to the Tower Clock a few yards away.

Then he continued his walk with slow dignity.

William stood staring after him sternly. In imagination he had reassumed the character of the late magnificent chief in order to deal with the policeman, and the policeman was pleading abjectly to him for his life. William treated the policeman to some of his famous ruthlessness, before he finally pardoned him. His self-respect restored by this proceeding, William went on down the promenade. He met Ethel again with the immaculate youth and pulled his most hideous grimace at them. The immaculate youth drew himself up, outraged and affronted, and Ethel passed on with an angry, glassy stare. William knew that Ethel would disclaim all knowledge of him and then would live in terror of the immaculate youth's discovering that he was her brother. Between William and Ethel there existed a state of continual warfare. What Ethel gained in the authority that accrued to her added years she lost by that respect for appearances that frequently laid her at William's mercy, and so they were about equally matched as adversaries. Uplifted in spirit by his encounter, William turned off the promenade into one of the crowded streets that led to it. At the end of it he saw a policeman regulating the traffic. He was the policeman of one's dreams. He radiated kindness and sympathy in every glance and movement. William felt that this was the one policeman of all the policemen in the world in whom he must confide his story of the spy. Narrowly escaping death beneath the wheels of several cars, he crossed the road to the middle, where the policeman, waving on one line of traffic and holding up another, looked down at him and said, "You'll cross the street like that once too often one day, my lad."

William, however, had not come to discuss his methods of crossing streets.

"There's a spy down on the beach," he said breathlessly, "he's been measuring it out an' making a map ready for the next war. You'll catch him if you're quick."

The policeman looked down at him, still kindly and amused.

"Now, my lad, don't try any of your funny work on me, because I haven't time for it."

Whereupon he held up the traffic for William to continue his passage of the street. Disconcerted, William continued it. He stood doubtfully on the further pavement, wondering what to do next. He was convinced that, if this policeman wouldn't believe him, none would. And the responsibility of bringing his spy to justice had begun to weigh heavily upon his spirit. He wandered slowly back to the shore, climbed into the unattended boat again and sat there thinking. As he scowled out over the sea, his head between his hands, he uttered his famous sardonic laugh. He knew why they wouldn't believe him. They thought of him as a child. They'd no idea what he really was. If he could get a grown-up to see what the spy was doing, it would be all right. The policeman would believe a grown-up. They always believed grown-ups.

"Now then!" said a voice behind him, "Nip out o' this an' look sharp."

William turned. The boatman to whom the boat belonged had come upon him unawares. He was a large man with a red face and a twinkle in his eye that belied his fierce voice.

" 'Less of course," he went on with obvious sarcasm, "you're wantin' a row an' willin' to pay for it."

And then suddenly the idea came to William. Here was his witness, the grown-up who should catch the spy red-handed and give him over to the police. The spy would be keeping a lookout upon the land, of course, but he worked with his back to the sea and he wouldn't be prepared for anyone coming upon him from that quarter.

"If you found a spy spyin'," said William, "would you give him up to the police?"

"You bet," said the man, winking at the breaker for want of anything else to wink at. "Why, I've caught dozens of 'em in my time."

William felt in his pocket. There reposed in it a sixpence that his father had given him that morning.

"Yes, I'll have a sail," said William, "a sixpenny one. Please."

"How far d'you think you'll get for sixpence?" said the man scornfully.

"I'll get as far as I want to get," said William, "an' I'll jolly well show you somethin' that you didn't know was there."

There seemed to be no other prospective customer in sight, so the man good-naturedly pushed off his boat and jumped into it. William watched him with envy. He had often wanted to do that. Once he got this spy business over, he'd see if he could learn how to do it. It probably wasn't as hard as it looked. There were lots of unattended boats along the beach that he could practise on.

"Well, where d'you want to go?" said the man.

"Keep close along the coast," said William, "it's jus' round that big rock – thc bit you can't see from here."

The boatman, thinking rightly that William would be a credulous audience, began to tell him about the sea serpents he had seen in his youth, but William's response was half-hearted. He was living for the moment when they should steal upon the spy from behind, and catch him engaged upon his nefarious work. Then there was that next and just-as-thrilling moment to think about, when the burly boatman should hand him over to the police, and William should tell how he had shadowed him and finally caught him.

"Round this 'ere point, did you say?" asked the boatman.

"Yes."

"You can't land there, you know, now," said the boatman, "it's high tide."

At that moment they rounded the point, and there, clinging in terror to the rocks, waist high in water, was the professor. As soon as he saw William and the boat, he gave a shout of joy.

"My rescuer!" he cried, "my noble rescuer!"

It was the next day. William was walking along the sea coast to the line of rocks beyond the beach. He had spent last evening in a blaze of glory. The professor had told the story eloquently to everyone in the boarding house. "This boy was playing about near me while I was working, and I sent him away because it worries me to have boys playing about near me when I'm working. He went away and later on he noticed that I had not returned, and, knowing that it would be high tide and that the rocks where I had been working would be covered (a fact that I had foolishly omitted to ascertain), the brave boy quietly hired a boat to come to my rescue. He saved my life . . ."

William, who was beginning to have a dim suspicion that the professor was not a spy after all, saw no reason to contradict the story. If the notoriety of having captured a dangerous spy were denied one, that of having rescued a celebrated professor of geology was better than nothing. He received the plaudits of the boarding house with modest nonchalance.

"Oh, that's nothin'," he said, "I'd do that for anyone any time. Savin' a person from drownin's nothin'."

To mark his gratitude the professor presented William with a ticket to a lecture that he was giving in the town that evening on Geology. William went to it, and it confirmed his suspicions that the professor was not a spy, because he was sure that no spy could make quite as dull a speech as the professor made. Further to mark his gratitude, the professor gave William's mother five pounds to add to William's post office savings account.

THEY ROUNDED THE POINT, AND THERE, CLINGING TO THE ROCKS, WAS THE PROFESSOR.

William thanked him perfunctorily. William looked upon his post office savings account as a deliberate scheme of his parents to divert from him any money that might come his way.

But it was now the next morning, and everyone, William included, was beginning to forget that he had saved the professor from a watery grave the day before. William was tired of being a secret service agent. He had decided to be a spy. He was an English spy in a foreign land. He had a piece of tape, stolen from his mother's

"MY RESCUER!" HE CRIED. "MY NOBLE RESCUER."

work bag, and a piece of stick to represent a hammer. With them he measured and tapped the rocks, stopping occasionally to scrawl hieroglyphics on a piece of paper. Sometimes imaginary natives of the place would pass, and William would slip the tokens of his trade into his pocket and talk to them volubly in their own language, explaining that he was a professor of geology. He brought all the foreign words he knew into these conversations. "*Hic, hœc, hoc,*" he would say, "*Je suis, tu es, il est, mensa mensa mensam, la plume de ma tante, dominus domine dominum . . .*"

After a short conversation of this sort the imagined foreigners would pass on their way, completely deceived, and William would return to his tapping and measuring.

He was perfectly happy . . .

CHAPTER NINE

WILLIAM AND THE UNFAIR SEX

WILLIAM WANDERED disconsolately down to the beach. His family had come to the sea for their summer holiday, and so far (they had arrived the day before) William was not amused. His father had set off for the golf course directly after breakfast. Robert and Ethel had joined a tennis set in the hotel garden. Mrs Brown was sitting in the lounge, learning the art of "quilting" from another visitor and thinking how nice it was not to have to think about lunch. William had spent an enjoyable half-hour experimenting first with the lift and then with the revolving doors, and had finally been forbidden to use either unattended. An electrician was now at work on the lift, and the old gentleman who had been carried round the revolving doors six times in William's whirlwind wake had been with difficulty persuaded not to sue the management for damages.

"No one stops *them* enjoying themselves," muttered William. "*They* go about havin' a good time all the time, but the minute I start they all get mad at me."

The absence of other children at the hotel added to his grievances.

"Lot of sick'nin' ole grown-ups," he muttered. "Lot

of sick'nin' ole grown-ups with nothin' to do 'cept talk newspaper stuff an' stop other people havin' a good time. Nice sort of holiday with a lot of sick'nin' ole grown-ups who . . ."

He stood looking down at the beach and his gloom increased. It was a sunless chilly morning and only two little girls were there.

"*Girls!*" he ejaculated scornfully. "Rott'n ole *girls!* Sickenin' ole grown-ups an' rott'n ole girls! You'd think there was a sort of *famine* of boys. You'd think someone'd killed 'em all off . . ."

His first thought was to walk away in disgust, but the little girls were about his own age and were in any case preferable to the grown-ups at the hotel. He watched them uncertainly . . . They were dressed alike in grey skirts and white blouses, and they were both hunting for shells, which they put into cardboard boxes, yet, despite the similarity of their clothing and pursuits, they worked at opposite ends of the beach and never spoke to each other. Slowly William went down the short sloping path to the beach. There he pretended to be deeply interested in the rocks and seaweed at the foot of the cliff. One of the little girls drew nearer in her search for shells till she was within hailing distance. Then she stood upright and said: "Hello."

William started and looked at her as if seeing her for the first time. He frowned as if interrupted in a pressing matter of business.

"Hello," he said distantly, and turned to study the cliff face again with an air of expert knowledge, pulling out bits of loose rock, examining them intently, then putting them back again.

The little girl watched him with interest, then said:

"What are you doing?"

William, who hadn't the faintest idea what he was doing, did not reply. Instead he countered aloofly: "What are *you* doing?"

"I'm collecting shells," said the little girl, holding out the cardboard box. "Look."

William looked. Yellow shells, blue shells, white shells, black shells. It was an impressive collection. But William carefully maintained his pose of bored detachment as he said:

"What are you collectin' 'em for?"

"I'M COLLECTING SHELLS," SAID THE LITTLE GIRL, HOLDING OUT THE CARDBOARD BOX.

The little girl's face shone suddenly.

"For Miss Twemlow," she said on a note of deep reverence.

"Who's she?" said William.

"Our form mistress," said the little girl on a note of still deeper reverence. "She's set us a holiday competition."

"And is that what your sister's doing, too?" asked William.

The little girl's expression changed from reverence to an almost venomous hatred.

"My sister? *That* awful girl? She's not my sister. I hate her. I'll never speak to her if I can help it."

"Then why have you got the same clothes on?" demanded William.

"It's our school uniform," said the little girl bitterly. "I *hate* going about in the same clothes as that awful girl, but it's the school uniform. She goes to the same school an' she lives here, too. I've begged and *begged* my mother to get me different clothes to wear in the holiday so that I needn't look the same as that awful girl, but she won't."

"Why don't you like her?" said William.

The little girl's face grew tense.

"It's because of Miss Twemlow," she said. "She used to be my best friend before Miss Twemlow came to the school. But last term she played the meanest trick on me. The meanest trick I've ever heard of."

"What was it?" said William with interest.

The little girl lowered her voice confidentially.

"Miss Twemlow had promised to let me sit by her at the half term lecture. She'd *promised* . . . I was having a music lesson just before and couldn't get in till just before the lecture began, and Angela – she's that awful girl – *knew* that Miss Twemlow had said I could sit next to her, and she went and sat next to her and wouldn't move when I came. Miss Twemlow never remembers who she's promised, and it's a matter of honour with us to let the one she promised first sit there."

William was silent for a moment, digesting this startlingly novel aspect of school life. On the few occasions on which he had sat next to a master at a lecture it had been because he had been forcibly dragged there from the seclusion of the back row, where his activities were proving a rival attraction to the lecture itself.

"Crumbs!" he said at last. "It mus' be jolly different at a girls' school."

"And it's not the first time she's played a trick like that on me," went on the little girl indignantly. "You can't trust her an inch . . . Not an inch."

She stared across the beach at the other figure in grey skirt and white blouse that was wandering to and fro, occasionally stopping to pick something up from the sand.

"Is she gettin' shells now?" asked William.

The little girl's expression grew yet more tense.

"Yes. She's in Miss Twemlow's form, too. And Miss Twemlow's quite nice to her – I can't think why, because she's an awful girl. An *awful* girl! But, of course," the ferocity of the little girl's expression softened to one of rapt and languishing sentimentality, "Miss Twemlow's so kind she'd be nice to anyone, however awful they were. She's so kind. And so beautiful." The little girl's expression was by now one of fatuous imbecility. "She's the most beautiful person who's ever lived. And clever, too. She can read things in the original language and that sort of thing. And she's got the most beautiful voice. In 'God save the King' you hear it above all the others. Just like an angel. She *looks* like an angel, too. I used to think Miss Folkat was an angel, before Miss Twemlow came, but – well, there's no comparison. Miss Twemlow's – well, I should think she's *more* beautiful than an angel . . ."

William listened with growing bewilderment, feeling vaguely glad that such emotional tangles did not complicate the simple lawlessness of his own school life.

"In a way," the little girl was saying, "she's like Norma Shearer, but in a way she's more beautiful. Do you know what I mean?"

William, however, was tired of discussing the unknown Miss Twemlow. He looked at the collection of shells and said:

"How many have you got?"

"Nearly two hundred," said the little girl proudly. "I keep them at home, of course. These are just the ones I've found today." She looked across at the other little girl and said wistfully: "I'd love to know how many Angela's got."

"Why don't you ask her?" said William.

"*Ask* her?" repeated the little girl, registering exaggerated horror and disgust. "Good gracious! I wouldn't ask her *anything*. Not if I was dying. Not after the way she behaved over that concert. I've not spoken to her since, and I wouldn't – not if she went down on her bended knees and begged me to . . . I say, I wish you'd go and ask her. Don't say it from me, of course. Just ask her how many she's got. Just as if you wanted to know yourself. You needn't stay with her, of course, because she's an *awful* girl."

"All right," said William, who was becoming rather bored and wanted to see what the other little girl was like. "I'll go an' ask her how many she's got."

"Yes," said the little girl anxiously, "and see if she's got an orange one. I can't find an orange one. Plenty of yellow, but not orange, and I know people *do* find orange ones here. Don't tell her I want to know, of course. Just find out if she's got one. I'm trying to find a blue stone, too, to have it polished and made into a brooch for Miss Twemlow. She's got blue eyes. She—"

But William, feeling that he couldn't bear to hear any more about Miss Twemlow for the present, was setting briskly off to the other little girl at the farther end of the beach. He slackened his pace as he neared her, wondering how to introduce himself, but she forestalled him, raising an earnest face from her search to say:

"What's your name?"

"William," said William. "I know yours. It's Angela."

She looked exactly like the other little girl, except that she was dark whereas the other little girl was fair.

"You've been with that *awful* Adela," said Angela, with a note of severity in her voice. "Don't believe anything she says. She's the most *awful* story teller. I don't know how you could *bear* to speak to her. She used to be my best friend, but that was before I really knew her. She played me the meanest trick!"

"What did she do?" said William.

"She found Miss Twemlow's places in chapel when it was my turn. She missed her turn with having a bilious attack, but that wasn't my fault. She knew Wednesday was my day, and when I went to find the hymns and lessons in Miss Twemlow's place she'd found them and put in the markers and she couldn't deny it because Lucy Masters *saw* her doing it. Have you ever *heard* of a meaner trick?"

William, who had heard of several, said nothing, and the little girl continued:

"I haven't spoken to her since, and I won't. I wouldn't speak to her, not – not even if the end of the world came. She knows why, too. She must have about the guiltiest conscience of anyone in the world. Wednesday's been my day ever since Miss Twemlow—"

"Yes," interrupted William. "She told me all about her."

"She doesn't *know* about her," said Angela passionately. "Miss Twemlow's only nice to her out of kindness. Miss Twemlow's so kind that—"

"Yes," said William hastily, "she told me all about that, too. How many shells have you got?"

"Nearly two hundred," said Angela. "How many has she?"

"Nearly two hundred," said William. "Have you got an orange one?"

"Has she?" said the little girl warily.

"No, have you?"

"No," admitted Angela. "I've got heaps of yellow ones, but I can't find an orange one anywhere. I know there are some, 'cause someone found one here . . . Will you help me look?"

William considered. He did not find either Adela or Angela stimulating company, but there didn't seem anything else to do.

"Well . . ." he said vaguely.

"I'll tell you a *wonderful* thing Miss Twemlow once did—" began Angela, but William interrupted.

"No, thanks," he said firmly. "I don't want to hear anythin' more about her. Tell you what. The other one – Adela – wants an orange shell, too, so I'll go off an' look for one an' if I find it, you can toss for it. How's that?"

Angela looked a little sulky.

"All right," she said, "if you won't look for me."

"Well, she wants one, too," said William, "so it's quite fair."

"All right," said Angela, thinking it was better than nothing, "but if you give it to *her* I'll never forgive you."

"I'll give it to the one the toss comes to," said William. "The first one, that is. An' I'll give the next to the other. I bet I find lots."

He took up his position conscientiously between the two of them and began to look for shells. Those he found he divided and took half each to his new friends, with apologies for the absence of an orange one.

"I bet I find one nex' time," he said. "I'm jolly good at findin' things."

If he'd found one he'd have left the little girls altogether and betaken himself to more congenial pursuits, but he was a boy who never liked to abandon any project unfinished. He'd undertaken to find an orange shell and he meant to do it . . . Moreover, as time went on, a sort of zest seized him. He found ten shells, twenty, thirty . . . and, though he still didn't find an orange one, Adela and Angela were separately very grateful to him for his contributions. The only drawback was that all topics of conversation led with a sort of diabolical fatality straight to Miss Twemlow and her perfections . . .

Going to bed that night, he decided that the whole thing was a waste of time and that in future he would avoid both Adela and Angela and their shell-hunting ground.

"As if I'd got nothin' else to do," he muttered to himself indignantly, "but look for orange shells!"

As a matter of fact, however, he *had* nothing else to do, and the next morning, after an unsuccessful attempt to explore the kitchen regions of the hotel, out of which he was chased by a temperamental Italian chef, he turned his feet slowly and almost reluctantly in the direction of the beach. He determined to find two orange shells and to reconcile Adela and Angela. They both liked talking about Miss Twemlow, so it would be much better for them to talk to each other about her than to him. He wasn't interested in Miss Twemlow. He imagined her, in fact, as a mixture of Violet Elizabeth Bott and a Pantomime Dame. But he quite liked Adela and Angela, in spite of their limited conversational powers, and wanted them to be able to talk to each other about Miss Twemlow. He thought they'd enjoy it . . . Now that they wouldn't let him experiment with the lift or the revolving doors or explore the kitchen, there seemed nothing to do but find an orange shell and reconcile Angela and Adela. He'd never reconciled anyone before and it would be a novel experience . . . The morning, however, was unsuccessful. He didn't find an orange shell and he didn't reconcile Adela and Angela. He took his "finds" to each in turn as he had done the previous day and put in a certain amount of not very subtle reconciliation propaganda, which did not enhance his own popularity.

"Wouldn't you like to talk to *her* about Miss

Twemlow?" he said to Adela. "*She* likes talkin' about her, too."

"*Her!*" ejaculated Adela fiercely. "I'm never going to speak to her again. I've *sworn* it. And Miss Twemlow can't know her as I do or *she* wouldn't speak to her, either. Haven't you found an orange shell yet?"

"No," said William, "not an orange one. I keep finding other colours."

"Has *she* got an orange one?"

"Why don't you go an' ask her," said William, "an' have a nice talk about – about Miss Twemlow an' things?"

"Never!" said Adela dramatically, and, pleased with the effect, repeated, still more dramatically: "*Never!*"

Angela was just as uncompromising.

"Speak to her! What should I speak to her about?"

"Miss Twemlow," suggested William.

"Speak to *her* about Miss Twemlow?" said Angela fiercely. "Why, Miss Twemlow—"

"All right," said William, returning to his no man's land to look for an orange shell.

If it hadn't been for the orange shell he certainly wouldn't have gone down to the beach again after lunch, but he wasn't going to be beaten by a little thing like an orange shell. Moreover, all the other members of his family had gone out, refusing to take him with them, and an old gentleman, roused from his after-lunch nap by his whistling, had been so disagreeable that William felt there was nothing for it but to go down to the beach again. No one seemed to want him but the little girls. Perhaps the little girls didn't exactly *want* him, but at any rate they endured his company in the hopes of an orange shell . . .

As soon as he reached the beach, Adela greeted him excitedly.

"She's *here*," she said.

"Who?" said William blankly.

"Miss Twemlow," said Adela. "I've *seen* her . . . I've *spoken* to her. She's *staying* here . . . I hope Angela hasn't seen her. I shan't tell her she's here."

At this moment Angela came running down the slope to the beach. She, too, looked flushed and excited. She beckoned William to her and spoke in a mysterious whisper.

"Don't tell Adela, but *she's* here. She's staying here. I've just spoken to her. Oh, William, she's more beautiful than ever."

"Where is she?" said William, interested despite himself.

"She's just going to her hotel at the end of the promenade. She's in a dark blue coat. You can't miss her. Do go and look at her, William. I can't tell you how beautiful she is . . ."

William went up to the promenade and hurried to overtake the figure in the dark blue coat at the other end. He was vaguely gratified to find that Miss Twemlow was a very ordinary-looking woman, with short-sighted peering eyes, wearing a coat several inches longer than the fashionable length.

The next morning, however, the little girls' ardour was damped.

"Her financé's here," said Adela morosely. "At least he's not here, but he's staying five miles away, and he's going to come over by train every day. She won't come to tea with me. She won't even come for a walk. She says she would if her fiancé wasn't here. It's rotten luck, isn't it?"

"Well, I don't know . . ." said William.

"Of course it's rotten luck," said Adela hotly. "Suppose *your* favourite schoolmaster was here and you found that he couldn't come to tea because his fiancée was here, too, what would you feel like?"

"Gosh!" ejaculated William faintly, but before he could make any effort to describe his own attitude to his instructors, she went on:

"Anyway, she's coming to the Conservative Fête tomorrow. Perhaps he won't come to that. I do hope he doesn't come. I'm almost certain to get the wild flowers prize. I did last year. And I'd love her to see me getting it . . ."

"What wild flowers prize?" said William.

"I'm a Junior Conservative," said Adela importantly, "and there's a competition for arranging wild flowers. And they give a prize from the platform. And if she was there without her stupid old fiancé it would be *glorious.* 'Cause she'd see my wild flowers and prize and everything. And I'd ask her to have tea with me. And she would if *he* wasn't there . . . I say, do go and find out from that awful Angela if she's had the cheek to ask her to tea."

William made his way across the beach to Angela, who was kicking the sand about in a disconsolate fashion.

"He's here," she greeted William. "I shan't get a chance of seeing her with *him* here. He's coming over by train every day. She won't even come to tea . . . And I was so excited when I heard she was coming to the Conservative Fête tomorrow, but she says *he's* coming too, so that means she won't have a minute for anything else."

"Are you going in for that wild flower thing?" asked William.

"Good gracious, no!" said Angela with fierce contempt. "I leave that rubbish to that awful Adela. But my cousin's going to open the fête. At least he's a sort of cousin. His father's a cabinet minister and *he* was going to come but he can't, so his son's coming. He's a second or third cousin or something like that. But I've met him, and I'd be able to introduce him to Miss Twemlow and he'd have an ice cream or something with us. I know he would. But, of course, if her fiancé's there, too, it wouldn't be any fun. She doesn't take any interest in anything when her fiancé's there. Oh, I wish I could *stop* him coming."

She was a much more attractive little girl than Adela. For one thing she was dark, and William had never preferred blondes. For another she had a wistful, drooping mouth, whereas Adela's was firm and somewhat aggressive.

"I'll stop him coming for you, if you like," said William.

The statement astonished him as much as it did Angela. He didn't know he was going to say it till he'd actually heard himself saying it.

She stared at him.

"You couldn't," she said.

William gave a slightly uneasy laugh.

"Oh yes, I could," he said, sticking to his guns. "Wouldn't be anythin' to me, that wouldn't."

"But *how* could you?" she persisted.

"Oh, I've got ways," he said mysteriously. "I've got ways, all right."

"But what ways?"

"I – I can't tell you," hedged William, "but I've got 'em. I've got a – sort of *power* over people."

Her incredulity was fading into puzzled admiration.

"Oh, William," she said, "have you? Why didn't you tell me before?"

"There were reasons," said William. "I – well, I don't like people to know about this power I've got."

"I suppose they'd always be wanting you to do things?" said Angela.

"Yes," said William, thankfully accepting the explanation, "they'd always be wanting me to do things. But I'll do this for you, all right. I don't mind doin' this for you."

Angela's dark eyes shone with gratitude, and William preened himself in it, putting off the evil hour when he must make good his rash undertaking.

"It's wonderful of you," she was saying, and added, "if you really can."

"Oh, I can, all right," said William.

"He's coming by the 2.15 train," said Angela. Sudden anxiety clouded the eagerness of her dark eyes. "You won't – wreck the train, will you, William?"

"N-no," promised William, as if somewhat reluctantly. "No, if you don't want me to do that, I won't."

"I don't want anyone killed."

"All right," conceded William generously. "All right, I won't kill anyone."

"I jus' want him kept away. Quite kindly, I mean."

"I'll be as kind as I can," said William darkly. "One's

gotter be a *bit* rough, doin' things like that. I always do 'em as kindly as I can."

"Oh, *William*!" said Angela. "Have you often kidnapped people?"

The awestruck admiration in her dark eyes went to William's head. He looked round in an exaggeratedly furtive manner.

"I'd better not tell you the things I've done," he said in a hoarse whisper. "I've done some things that – well, I'd jus' better not tell you 'em, that's all."

"You mean – you mean – the sort of things you read about in the newspaper?" said Angela breathlessly.

"Yes," said William, glad to have the details of his supposed crimes left to the imagination. "Yes, the sort you read in the papers."

The little girl heaved a deep sigh of mingled relief and ecstasy.

"I shan't worry a *bit* now," she said. "I *know* he won't be there and that I shall have a lovely time with Miss Twemlow and my cousin. That awful Adela'll be *mad*. She doesn't know my cousin, and I shan't introduce her."

It didn't occur to William till he was on his way to the station the next afternoon that he had never seen Miss Twemlow's fiancé and so would not be able to recognise him when he arrived. But the reflection did not worry him for long. There probably wouldn't be many young men and he'd ask them all. Angela's admiration had made him look on himself as a superman . . . A little obstacle like that was nothing to him. When the train steamed in he was relieved to see that only one young man descended from it. He was an amiable-looking young man with a slightly receding chin, slightly protruding eyes and a vague but eminently friendly smile. After one glance at him, William felt convinced that he couldn't be anyone but Miss Twemlow's fiancé. He had decided, however, that it might arouse his suspicions to ask him straight out if he were Miss Twemlow's fiancé. He had evolved a more subtle method of approach. He went up to the young man and, assuming a stern businesslike expression, said:

" 'Scuse me. Are you goin' to the 'servative Fête?"

The young man brightened. He suggested a lost dog who has suddenly sighted its owner.

"Yes," he said. "Yes, that's where I'm bound, my young friend."

"Well, they sent me to show you the way," said William.

The young man's smile became brighter still.

"Jolly good of them!" he said. "Jolly good of them! Well, shall we start wending? The sooner it's over, the sooner to sleep, what?"

William found this calm unquestioning acceptance of the situation a little disconcerting. He had expected to have to use finesse, but apparently no finesse was demanded of him. He felt even a little disappointed. It was turning out almost too simple . . .

"All right," he said. "Come on."

He was relieved to find that Miss Twemlow's fiancé did not know where the fête was to be held and that his carefully prepared and somewhat involved explanation – that the ground had been flooded during the night and the site had had to be changed – would not be necessary. (In view of the fact that it had not rained during the night he had felt that it might be difficult to sustain.) He steered Miss Twemlow's fiancé into a road that led in the opposite direction to that of the fête. Miss Twemlow's fiancé quite happily allowed himself to be steered.

"Hope I'm not late," he said.

"Oh, no," said William, "you're not late."

"Not too fond of these things, don't you know," Miss Twemlow's fiancé confessed, "but needs must when the devil drives, what?"

"Yes," said William, supposing that he meant Miss Twemlow by the devil.

When they had been walking for some time, William considered his next step. Miss Twemlow's fiancé was so far unsuspicious, but if they went on walking indefinitely his suspicions were bound to be aroused sooner or later. He had in fact already said, "About five minutes' walk from the station, isn't it?" and they had now been walking for at least ten.

"Nearly there, I suppose, aren't we, what?" he said suddenly, and William realised that something must be done at once or even this very trusting and gullible young man might begin to smell a rat. They turned a bend in the road, and there on a large open space by the roadside a fair was in progress. Merry-go-rounds went merrily round, swings swung to dizzy heights, showmen shouted and music blared. William clutched at the straw.

"Here we are," he said. "Here's the fête . . ."

He looked at the young man apprehensively, but his credulity was evidently still unstrained.

"Good!" he said. "Quite a jolly walk! But now to business, what?" and turned in at the entrance of the fair. Inside, he stood and looked round with evident approval.

"I say, this is jolly. No starch about this, what? Sort of thing I like, don't you? Can't stand starch, what?"

William heaved a sigh of relief and entered the fair-ground with his companion. His companion's approval increased as they wandered round the booths and swings.

"Jolly well arranged," he said. "No one fussing you all the time. Hate being fussed, what?"

He looked about him as he walked. Looking for Miss Twemlow, probably, thought William.

"Miss Twemlow said she might be late," he said, taking the bull by the horns.

"That's a pity," said the young man vaguely, "but I suppose it can't be helped, what?"

He didn't seem very sorry that Miss Twemlow might be late, and, remembering Miss Twemlow, William couldn't feel surprised by this.

They had reached a small platform upon which normally a Strong Man challenged passers-by to a boxing bout. The Strong Man, however, had vanished at the moment in search of a quick one, and the Strong Man's wife, resplendent in purple dress and plentifully be-feathered hat, sat on the platform fanning herself with her hand.

"I suppose that's Lady Cynthia," said Miss Twemlow's fiancé uncertainly. "Never met any of them before, you know. Bit awkward in its way. Still, England expects, what?"

With an expansive smile he approached the feathered lady and wrung her hand.

"How d'you do, Lady Cynthia," he said. "So glad to see you. Hope I'm not late."

The feathered lady gave a scream of delight and swung his hand up and down.

"How d'you do, Sir Harchibald," she replied. "*Sow* good of you to come!"

"Not at all," deprecated Miss Twemlow's fiancé. "Only too glad. Well, shall we get on with the good work, what?"

He leapt upon the platform and began in a high-pitched nervous voice. "Ladies and gentlemen . . ."

The small crowd that had gathered to witness his greeting of the Strong Man's wife cheered, and others joined the crowd.

"I'm afraid I'm not much of a speaker," said Miss Twemlow's fiancé, "but I'll do my best."

Loud cheers greeted this. The orator looked gratified and continued:

"Well, I'm sure you don't want to waste any more time listening to me (Louder cheers) so I'll just declare this Sale of Work open and hope you'll all have a thoroughly enjoyable afternoon. Empty your purses and the stalls, what? On with the dance, let joy be unconfined, don't you know. And never forget that it's the Conservative party that made jolly old England what it is."

Wild applause broke out on all sides, and, blushing with pleasure, the orator leapt down from the platform, shook hands with the feathered lady, who was rocking with mirth, then set off through the crowd with William.

"That went off all right, don't you think?" he said complacently. "A jolly good audience, what? Mind you, I'm not a speaker. When I have to speak, my motto is 'Short and to the point.' That went down quite well, didn't it? Jolly old bird, Lady Cynthia. I always find those *nouveaux riches* easy to get on with. No starch, what? The old bird got my name wrong, but I can never remember names myself. Always dropping bricks with people's names."

The report that a new humorist had arrived on the scene spread far and wide, and a crowd was now accompanying them round the fair. William, too, had enjoyed the joke. Everything in fact seemed to be going swimmingly.

"Got to do our duty and buy something, I suppose," Miss Twemlow's fiancé was saying. "Not so many of these so-called fancy stalls as usual, what? An improvement on the usual thing all round. Never been to one with less starch. Jolly good idea, what?"

He paused at the next stall and watched a man who was demonstrating pull-out toffee, pulling it out to the length of his arm like elastic and clapping it together again. Miss Twemlow's fiancé bought two pounds of it, which the man wrapped in a brown paper parcel. He then wandered on to a hoopla stall, where, more by good luck than good management, he won an enormous vase of hideous design. Most of the crowd, disappointed by his failure to live up to his reputation as a humorist, had left him, but a small remnant was still faithful, and loudly cheered his winning of the vase. Miss Twemlow's fiancé was obviously enjoying himself. He continued to comment expansively on the unexpected absence of "starch".

"No idea it would be like this," he said. "Thought I'd have to pace round with a lot of bally old dowagers, buying tea cosies and saying polite what-nots. Always stumps me, that. Never know what to say to people. This is a reform, my young friend, that's long overdue, and I congratulate your little community down here on having thought of it. No doubt it will spread to other places like wildfire. Ye gods! When I think of the torment I've endured with dowagers, polite converse and tea cosies . . . Come on, let's have a shy at a coconut."

Miss Twemlow's fiancé had an unexpectedly determined nature and, after the expenditure of one and sixpence in balls, succeeded in winning a coconut. He paid for William to try, but William was preoccupied and did himself less than justice. The situation could not, of course, be expected to continue at this stage indefinitely. Sooner or later the suspicions of the young man were bound to be aroused. Already he was evidently wondering in what capacity William had constituted himself his faithful bodyguard.

"I suppose you're Lady Cynthia's son, what?" he said carelessly.

"Gosh, no!" said William, then realised too late that it would have been safer to say "yes".

"Official of the Junior Branch, then, I suppose," said Miss Twemlow's fiancé, beaming at him. "Like the way they bring that to the fore these days. Youth at the helm, what? Perhaps that's why starch is on the wane. What about a ride on the gee-gees?"

William agreed. The church clock struck four. Well, at any rate, he thought, Adela and Angela would have had a clear hour with Miss Twemlow while he kept her fiancé at bay. Adela would have got the wild flowers prize, Angela would have introduced her to her cousin and he would have had an ice with them. They ought to be jolly grateful to him. He was getting a little tired of Miss Twemlow's fiancé, however, and thought he'd take him back to the station now as soon as possible. He must find some excuse, of course, for Miss Twemlow's non-appearance. Miss Twemlow's fiancé was climbing down from his wooden steed.

"Years since I went on a merry-go-round," he was saying happily. "What about a glass of lemonade?" They each drank a glass of synthetic liquid of a rich golden colour, which Miss Twemlow's fiancé pronounced excellent. Then William said:

"Well, I s'pose it's time you went back."

Miss Twemlow's fiancé looked at his watch.

"By Jove, I suppose it is," he said. "I'd better go and find Lady Cynthia."

"No, I wouldn't do that," said William. "I wouldn't do that. Well, she told me to tell you that she was busy an' she sent a message to say goodbye."

"Oh, that's all right," said Miss Twemlow's fiancé, relieved. "Decent old dame, but all this social stuff gets on one's nerves. That's what I've enjoyed about this afternoon. No . . . no . . ." He searched for a word.

"Starch," supplied William.

"That's it, by Jove!" said the young man, delighted. "No starch."

"Well, we'd better be gettin' to the station now," said William. "I don't think Miss Twemlow's goin' to be here. She said she might not."

"Yes, sorry not to have met Miss Twemlow," said the young man vaguely.

"She sent you love and kisses," said William.

"Very kind of her," said the young man, slightly taken aback. "Very kind indeed."

They were now on their way to the station, and William was congratulating himself on the final success of his scheme, when an old lady appeared round the bend of the road. William recognised her as an old lady staying at his hotel but hoped himself to escape recognition, as she was not one of those many inmates of the hotel who had objected to his various activities, and with luck might not even have noticed him. He was walking past her with a blank expressionless face when she stopped and said:

"Why, it's William! I should have thought you'd have been at the fête, dear."

"We've been there," said William.

"Yes, by Jove!" put in Miss Twemlow's fiancé, pointing in the direction of the fair. "We've just come from it."

"I'm afraid you're mistaken," said the old lady. "The fête is in Sir Gerard Bannister's grounds about a quarter of a mile from here."

"By Jove!" said Miss Twemlow's fiancé. "You're joking!"

"I never joke," said the old lady. "I've just come from the fête myself! Good day."

She walked on. They stood staring after her.

"I say!" said Miss Twemlow's fiancé. "We can't have made a mistake, can we?"

"No," said William desperately. "She's batty. I know her. She's stayin' at our hotel. She's batty. They let her go about alone 'cause she's not dangerous. She's jus' batty. She tells people things are in places where they aren't, like what she did now. No one takes any notice of her. Don't you worry about her. You go on home same as you were goin' to."

But Miss Twemlow's fiancé's conscience had evidently been roused. His bright all-embracing smile had faded. He looked worried.

"Think I'd better make sure," he said anxiously.

"Don't want to make a hash of things. Promised the old man I'd do it in style, what?"

"But I tell you she doesn't know what she's talkin' about," pleaded William. "No one ever takes any notice of what she says. She's all right 'cept about places. She doesn't know where they are. She says they're in places where they aren't, same as she did jus' now. She—"

A look of calm determination had come into the young man's face.

"Tell you what I'll do," he said. "It's quite early, so I'll just walk along a bit and make sure. The old man said I'd probably make a hash of things, and I don't want the old bean to be able to say, 'I told you so.' Must go home with a clean escutcheon, what? Nice little walk for us both, and we'll feel then that we've left no stone unturned, no avenue unexplored, as the poet saith."

"All right," said William, yielding to the inevitable.

After all, he told himself, it didn't really matter. It was nearly five o'clock. Adela and Angela would have had all the afternoon with Miss Twemlow. Again he thought complacently of their gratitude and admiration. He had indeed gloriously vindicated his "power over people".

The next bend in the road brought them to the main gate of Sir Gerard Bannister's park and showed them the Conservative Fête in full swing. Posters advertised it. Loudspeakers announced it. At that moment a military band struck up. The young man's mouth fell open.

"By Jove!" he said.

He looked round for William, but William was no longer to be seen. He was making his way through a small unauthorised opening in the palings into the park. He wanted to find Adela and Angela and receive their glowing thanks. He found Adela first. She was standing by herself, morosely watching a putting competition.

"Well," William greeted her complacently, "I kept him away all right, didn't I?"

She stared at him.

"Kept who away?" she demanded.

"Miss Twemlow's what-d'you-call-it," said William. "I kept him away, all right, didn't I?"

Her small face stiffened with anger.

"D'you think you're funny?" she asked in withering contempt.

It was William's turn to stare at her.

"Well, didn't I keep him away?" he challenged.

"Keep him away!" she echoed furiously. "He's been here all afternoon."

"He – but he couldn't have been," said the bewildered William. "I've been with him. I've kept him away . . . I've kept him away so's you would get your wild flowers prize an'—"

"Wild flowers prize!" she repeated. "They didn't even judge them, and *she* wouldn't have seen if I *had* got it 'cause *he* was there all the time."

The world seemed to spin round William.

"He – why didn't they judge them?"

" 'Cause the man who was going to open the fête and judge the wild flowers never turned up," said Adela venomously. "Never turned up. And they were all so worried what had happened to him that they didn't even get anyone else to do it. They said that we could have it again at one of the ordinary meetings. As if that's any good to me! I wanted *her* to see me get the prize, and she was talking to *him* all the time. I shouldn't have minded that so much if I'd got the prize. I could have showed it her, anyway. She'd have had to have *looked* at it and known I'd won it, but with that man that was going to judge them not turning up—"

"But look here," interrupted William. "He *can't* have been here. Miss Twemlow's what-d'you-call-it, I mean. He was with me all the time." He looked round. "Where is he? Show me him."

"He's gone," said Adela. "They've both gone. They went about five minutes ago."

"What was he like?" said William.

Adela stamped angrily.

"I'm sick of answering silly questions. What does it matter what he was like? You said you'd keep him away and you didn't. I've had a *horrible* afternoon, and it's all your fault."

"But listen," said William, "you must have made a mistake. You—"

Adela, however, refused to listen. She turned away from him impatiently and disappeared in the crowd.

Bewildered and apprehensive, William wandered off. Almost at once he came upon Angela. She was watching Bowling for a Live Pig with an air of suffering patience.

He accosted her cautiously:

"I say," he said, "I *did* stop him. I did, honest. I met him at the station an'—"

She swung round on him.

"You story teller!" she said. "He's been here all the time . . . You're just a *story* teller, that's what you are. Making out you can do things, an' all the time you can't."

"I'm not. I'm not, honest," pleaded William. "I did keep him away. Listen, I—"

"I've had a *miserable* afternoon," went on Angela. "My cousin didn't come at all. He was supposed to be opening it, but he never came at all. I shouldn't have minded *him* being here so much if my cousin had come, too. I could have introduced her to him, anyway, and he'd have given us an ice and that would have been better than *nothing*."

A horrible suspicion was taking form in William's mind. He looked about him. Standing near was a group of fashionably-dressed and worried-looking women, talking in agitated but lowered voices. He drew near to listen.

"But, my dear," one of them was saying, "I can't *think* what's happened. They say he caught the train at the other end. There's no doubt of that. And we've rung up the police and there haven't been any accidents. What on *earth* can have happened to him?"

At that moment William's companion of the afternoon could be seen making his way towards them. He still wore his radiant and all-embracing smile. He still carried his vase, his two coconuts and his parcel of pullout toffee.

"I say," he said, "I'm so terribly sorry. I've only just realised. I went to the wrong place. The boy—" His eye fell on William and his smile grew yet more radiant and all-embracing as he recognised him. "There he is! A jolly good little scout he is, too, but we went to the wrong show. He—"

It was at this point that William, throwing ceremony to the winds, turned and made good his escape.

*

It was the next morning. William walked jauntily along the promenade. He'd got up before breakfast and gone down to the beach and found two orange shells. *Two* orange shells . . . One, of course, would have caused a certain awkwardness, but two! . . . He'd made a little mistake yesterday (how could he have known that Miss Twemlow's fiancé was going to change his mind and come by car?) but the orange shells would put things right. Adela and Angela would be so grateful for the orange shells that they'd forget all about yesterday. He'd be a hero, a superman – a boy who could find two orange shells in five minutes when they'd been looking for them in vain for weeks. He hoped it would make them friends again. He wanted to make them friends before he went home. He'd got a piece of good news for them, too. Someone staying at the hotel knew Miss Twemlow and said that her fiancé had to go to London on business for the next two days. She'd be able to go for walks with Adela and Angela now and have tea with them. They'd be jolly grateful to him for finding that out . . .

He had felt a bit apprehensive after his mistake of yesterday but nothing had happened. The young man had so evidently enjoyed his visit to the Fair, and his account of the part William had played in the matter was so confused, that the authorities had decided to take no steps. He had probably asked the boy the way, they decided, and the boy, himself a stranger to the district, had thought he meant the fair . . . Not knowing William, they gave him the benefit of the doubt – a benefit that was seldom accorded to him in his home surroundings. He had spent an anxious evening, but no irate Conservative

WILLIAM, THROWING CEREMONY TO THE WINDS, TURNED AND MADE GOOD HIS ESCAPE.

arrived at the hotel to lay the case before his father, and this morning the danger of that was safely over. And he'd found two orange shells and had discovered that Miss Twemlow's fiancé was going away . . .

Suddenly he saw them coming along the promenade together. They were walking arm-in-arm. Obviously they

"I'M SO TERRIBLY SORRY. I'VE ONLY JUST REALISED. I WENT TO THE WRONG PLACE," SAID WILLIAM'S COMPANION.

had made friends. That was a good thing. They'd be easier to get on with together than several yards apart. He approached them with a triumphant smile and held out his palm, on which reposed the two orange shells.

"Look!" he said in serene confidence of their gratitude and delight.

They stared blankly, first at the shells and then at William.

"Well?" said Adela coldly.

"I – I – well, you *wanted* an orange shell, didn't you?" said William, taken aback.

The scene wasn't going at all as he'd imagined it going. He couldn't understand it . . . Where were the cries of delight, the "Oh, William, *thank* you. How clever of you."

"Good gracious!" said Angela with an affected laugh. "Fancy you remembering that! We did play with shells once, I remember, when we'd nothing else to do, but we found it very babyish and boring, didn't we, Adela?"

"My goodness, yes!" shrilled Adela. "Can't think what anyone *sees* in the things."

"Fancy a great boy like you wasting your time over them!" said Angela, looking with dramatic contempt from the shells in William's outstretched hand to William himself.

The world rocked round him.

"But listen," he pleaded. "Listen. He's goin' away – the what-d'you-call-it. She can come out to tea with you today an' tomorrow."

Adela's wide-open eyes registered amused bewilderment.

"Who on earth are you talking about?"

"Miss Twemlow," said William.

Two heads were tossed disdainfully, two peals of scornful laughter rang out.

"My *goodness*!" said Adela. "*That* woman!"

"As if," said Angela, "we ever wanted to see her again!"

"*Or* you," said Adela. "Come on, Angela, darling! Don't let's waste any more time."

They walked on. William stared after them open-mouthed. At the end of the short promenade they swung round and walked back. They still walked arm-in-arm, heads close together, talking in confidential undertones. As they passed William they lifted their noses in aloof disgust, but this time did not even look at him . . .

CHAPTER TEN

WILLIAM'S EVENING OUT

WILLIAM'S FAMILY had come up to London for a holiday. They had brought William with them chiefly because it was not safe to leave William behind. William was not the sort of boy who could be trusted to live a quiet and blameless life at home in the absence of his parents. He had many noble qualities, but he had not that one. So William gloomily and reluctantly accompanied his family to London.

William's elder sister and mother lived in a whirl of shopping and theatres; William's elder brother went every day to see a county cricket match, and returned in a state of frenzied excitement to discuss the play and players all the evening without the slightest encouragement from anyone; William's father foregathered with old cronies at his club or slept in a hotel smoking room.

It was open to William to accompany any of the members of his family. He might shop and attend matinées with his mother and Ethel, he might go (on sufferance) to watch cricket matches with Robert, or he might sleep in the smoking room with his father.

He was encouraged by each of them to join some other member of the family, and he occasionally managed to evade them all and spend the afternoon sliding down the banisters (till firmly, but politely, checked by the manager of the hotel), watching for any temporary absence of the liftman during which he might try to manipulate the machine himself, or contending with the most impudent-looking page-boy in a silent and furtive rivalry in grimaces. But, in spite of this, he was supremely bored. He regarded the centre of the British Empire with contempt.

"*Streets!*" he said, with devastating scorn, at the end of his first day there. "*Shops!* Huh!"

William's soul pined for the fields and lanes and woods of his home; for his band of boon companions, with whom he was wont to wrestle, and fight, and trespass, and plot daredevil schemes, and set the world at defiance; for the irate farmers who helped to supply that spice of danger and excitement without which life to William and his friends was unendurable.

He took his London pleasures sadly.

"Oh – *history!*" he remarked coldly, when they escorted him round Westminster Abbey. His only comment on being shown the Tower was that it seemed to be takin' up the whole day, not that there was much else to do, anyway.

His soul yearned for the society of his own kind. The son of his mother's cousin, who lived near, had come to see him one day. He was a tall, pale boy, who asked William if he could foxtrot, and if he didn't adore Axel Haig's etchings, and if he didn't prefer Paris to London. The conversation was an unsatisfactory one, and the acquaintance did not ripen.

But, accompanying his family on various short cuts in the back streets of London, he had glimpsed another world, a world of street urchins, who fought and wrestled, and gave vent to piercing whistles, and hung on to the backs of carts, and paddled in the gutter, and rang front-door bells and fled from policemen. He watched it wistfully. Socially, his tastes were not high. All he demanded from life was danger and excitement and movement and the society of his own kind. He liked boys, crowds of boys, boys who shouted and whistled and ran and courted danger, boys who had never heard of any silly old etchings.

As he followed his family with his air of patient martyrdom on all their expeditions, it was the glimpse of this underworld alone that would lift the shadow from his furrowed brow and bring a light to his stern, freckled countenance . . . There were times when he stopped and tried to get into contact with it, but it was not successful. His mother's "Come along, William. Don't speak to those horrid little boys" always recalled him to the blameless and palling respectability of his own family. Yet even before that hateful cry interrupted him he knew that it was useless.

He was an alien being – a clean little boy in a neat suit, with a fashionable mother and sister. He was beyond the pale, an outsider, a pariah, a creature to be mocked and jeered at. The position galled William. He was, by instinct, on the side of the lawless – the anti-respectable.

His spirits rose as the time for his return to the country approached. Yet there was a wistful longing at his heart for the boy world at London still unexplored, as well as a fierce contempt for the London his parents had revealed to him.

*

William had been invited to a party on his last evening in London. William's mother's cousin lived in Kensington, and had invited William to a "little gathering of her children's friends". William did not wish to go to the party. What is more, William did not intend to go to the party. But a wonderful plan had come into William's head.

"It's very kind of her," he said meekly. "Yes, I'll be very pleased to go."

This was unlike William's usual manner of receiving an invitation to a party. Generally there were expostulations, indignation, assertion of complete incapacity to go to anything that particular night. William's mother looked at him.

"You – you feel all right, don't you, dear?" she said anxiously.

"Oh, yes," said William, "an' I feel I'd jus' like a party."

"You can wear your Eton suit," said Mrs Brown.

"Oh, yes," said William. "I'd like that."

William's face was quite expressionless as he spoke. Mrs Brown pinched herself to make sure that she was awake.

"I expect they'll have music and dancing and that sort of thing," she said.

She thought, perhaps, that William had misunderstood the kind of party it would be.

William's expressionless face did not change.

"Oh, yes," he said pleasantly, "music and dancin' will be fine."

When Mr Brown was told of the invitation he groaned.

"And I suppose it will take the whole day to make him go," he said.

"No," said Mrs Brown eagerly. "That's the strange part. He seems to *want* to go. He really does. And he seems to *want* to wear his Eton suit, and you know what a bother that used to be. I suppose he's beginning to take a pride in his appearance. I think London must be civilising him."

"Well," said Mr Brown, dryly, "I suppose you know best. I suppose miracles do happen."

When the evening of the party arrived, there was some difficulty as to the transit of William to his place of entertainment. The house was so near to the hotel where the Browns were staying that a taxi seemed hardly worth while. But there was a general reluctance to be his escort.

Ethel was going to a theatre, and Robert had been out all day and thought he deserved a bit of rest in the evening, instead of carting kids about, Mrs Brown's rheumatism had come on again, and Mr Brown wanted to read the evening paper.

William, sleek and smooth, and brushed and encased in his Eton suit, his freckled face shining with cleanliness and virtue, broke meekly into the discussion.

"I know the way, mother. Can't I just go myself?"

Mrs Brown wavered.

"I don't see why not," she said at last.

"If you think that boy can walk three yards by himself without getting into mischief . . ." began Mr Brown.

William turned innocent, reproachful eyes upon him.

"Oh, but *look* at him," said Mrs Brown; "and it isn't as if he didn't want to go to the party. You want to go, don't you, dear?"

"Yes, mother," said William, meekly.

His father threw him a keen glance.

"Well, of course," he said, returning to his paper, "do as you like. I'm certainly not going with him myself, but don't blame me if he blows up the Houses of Parliament or dams the Thames, or pulls down Nelson's Monument."

William's sorrowful, wistful glance was turned again upon his father.

"I won't do any of those things, I promise, father," he said solemnly.

"I don't see why he shouldn't go alone," said Mrs Brown. "It's not far, and he's sure to be good, because he's looking forward to it so; aren't you, William?"

"Yes, mother," said William, with his most inscrutable expression.

So he went alone.

William set off briskly down the street – a neat figure in an Eton suit, an overcoat, a well-fitting cap and patent leather shoes.

His expression had relaxed as soon as the scrutiny of his family was withdrawn. It became expectant and determined.

Once out of the sight of possible watchers from the hotel, he turned off the road that led to his mother's cousin's house, and walked purposefully down a side street and thence to another side street.

There they were. He knew they would be there. Boys – boys after William's own heart – dirty boys, shouting boys, whistling boys, fighting boys. William approached. At his own home he would have been acclaimed at once as leader of any lawless horde. But here he was not known. His present appearance, moreover – brushed hair, evening clothes, clean face – was against him. To them he was a thing taboo. They turned on him with delightful yells of scorn.

"Yah!"

"Where's yer mammy?"

"Look at 'is shoes! Boo-oo!"

"*Isn't* 'is 'air brushed nice?"

"Yah!"

"Boo!"

"Garn!"

The tallest of them snatched William's cap from his head and ran off with it. The snatching of a boy's cap from his head is a deadly insult. William, whose one wistful desire was to be friends with his new acquaintances, yet had his dignity to maintain. He flew after the boy and caught him by the back of his neck. Then they closed.

The rest of the tribe stood round them in a ring, giving advice and encouragement. The contempt for William vanished. For William was a good fighter. He lost his collar and acquired a black eye; and his hair, in the exhilaration of the contest, recovered from its recent severe brushing and returned to his favourite vertical angle.

The two were fairly well matched, and the fight was a most satisfactory one till the cry of "Cops" brought it to an abrupt end, and the crowd of boys, with William now in the middle, fled precipitately down another street. When they were at a safe distance from the blue helmet, they stopped, and the large boy handed William his cap.

" 'Ere you *are*," he said, with a certain respect.

William, with a careless gesture, tossed the cap into the air. "Don't want it," he said.

"Wot's yer nime?"

"William."

" 'E's called Bill," said the boy to the others.

William read in their faces a growing interest, not quite friendship yet, but still not quite contempt. He glowed with pride. He put his hands into the pockets of his overcoat and there met – a sixpence – joy!

"Wot's your name?" he said to his late adversary.

" 'Erb," said the other, still staring at William with interest.

"Come on, 'Erb," said William jauntily, "let's buy some sweets, eh?"

He entered a small, unsavoury sweetshop, and the whole tribe crowded in after him. He and 'Erb discussed the rival merits of bulls' eyes and cokernut kisses at length.

"Them larses longer," said 'Erb, "but these 'ere tases nicer."

Finally, William airily tasted one of the cokernut kisses and the whole tribe followed his example – to be chased by the indignant shopkeeper all the way down the street.

"*Eatin*' of 'em!" he shouted furiously. "*Eatin*' of 'em without *payin*' for 'em. I'll set the cops on ye – ye young thieves."

They rushed along the next street shouting, whistling and pushing each other. William's whistle was louder than any, he ran the foremost. The lust of lawlessness was growing on him. They swarmed in at the next sweetshop, and William purchased sixpennyworth of bulls' eyes and poured them recklessly out of the bag into the grimy, outstretched palms that surrounded him.

William had no idea where he was. His hands were as

WILLIAM WAS HAPPY AT LAST. HE WAS A BOY AMONG BOYS — AN OUTLAW AMONG OUTLAWS.

THEY RUSHED ALONG THE NEXT STREET, SHOUTING AND WHISTLING.

grimy as the hands of his companions, his face was streaked with dirt wherever his hands had touched it, his eye was black, his collar was gone, his hair was wild, his overcoat had lost its look of tailored freshness. And he was happy at last.

He was no longer a little gentleman staying at a select hotel with his family. He was a boy among boys – an outlaw among outlaws once more. He was no longer a pariah. He had proved his valour in fighting and running and whistling. He was almost accepted, not quite. He was alight with exhilaration.

In the next street a watering cart had just passed, and there was a broad muddy stream flowing along the gutter. With a whoop of joy the tribe made for it, 'Erb at the head, closely followed by William.

William's patent leather shoes began to lose their damning smartness. It was William who began to stamp as he walked, and the rest at once followed suit – splashing, shouting, whistling, jostling, they followed the muddy stream through street after street. At every corner William seemed to shed yet another portion of the nice equipment of the boy-who-is-going-to-a-party. No party would have claimed him now – no hostess greeted him – no housemaid admitted him – he had completely "burned his boats". But he was happy.

All good things come to an end, however, even a muddy stream in a gutter, and 'Erb, still leader, called out: "Come on, you chaps! Come on, Bill – bells!"

Along both sides of a street they flew at breakneck speed, pulling every bell as they passed. Three enraged householders pursued them. One of them, fleeter than the other two, caught the smallest and slowest of the tribe and began to execute corporal punishment.

It was William who returned, charged from behind, left the householder winded in the gutter, and dragged the yelling scapegoat to the shelter of his tribe.

"Good ole Bill," said 'Erb, and William's heart

swelled again with pride. Nothing on earth would now have checked his victorious career.

A motor-van passed with another gang of street urchins hanging on merrily behind. With a yell of battle, William hurled himself upon them, struggled with them in mid-air, and established himself, cheering on his own tribe and pushing off the others.

In the fight William lost his overcoat, his Eton coat was torn from top to bottom, and his waistcoat ripped open. But his tribe won the day; the rival tribe dropped off, hurling ineffectual taunts and insults, and on sailed William and his gang, half-running, half-riding, with an exhilarating mixture of physical exercise and joy-riding unknown to the more law-abiding citizen.

And in the midst was William – William serene and triumphant, William dirty and ragged, William acclaimed leader at last. The motor-van put on speed. There was a ride of pure breathless joy and peril before, at last exhausted, they dropped off.

Then 'Erb turned to William: "Wot you doin' tonight, maite?" he said.

Maite! William's heart glowed.

"Nothin', maite," answered William carelessly.

"Oi'm goin' to the picshers," said 'Erb. "If you loike ter help my o'd woman with the corfee-stall, she'll give yer a tanner."

A coffee-stall – oh, joy! Was the magic of this evening inexhaustible?

"Oi'll 'elp 'er orl *roight*, maite," said William, making an effort to acquire his new friend's accent and intonation.

"Oi'll taike yer near up to it," said 'Erb, and to the gang: "Nah, you run orf 'ome, kids. Me an' Bill is busy."

He gave William a piece of chewing gum, which William proudly took and chewed and swallowed, and led him to a streetcorner, from where a coffee-stall could be seen in a glare of flaming oil-jets.

"You just say ''Erb sent me', an' you bet you'll get a tanner when she shuts up – if she's not in a paddy. Go on. Goo'-night."

He fled, leaving William to approach the stall alone. A large, untidy woman regarded him with arms akimbo.

"I've come ter 'elp with the stall," said William, trying to speak with the purest of Cockney accents. " 'Erb sent me."

The woman regarded him with a hostile stare, still with arms akimbo.

"Oh, 'e did, did 'e? 'E's allus ready ter send someone else. 'E's gone ter the picshers, I suppose? 'E's a nice son for a poor woman ter 'ave, isn't 'e? Larkin' abaht orl day an' goin' ter picshers orl night – an' where do *Oi* come in? I asks yer, where do *Oi* come in?"

William, feeling that some reply was expected, said that he didn't know. She looked him up and down. Her expression implied that her conclusions were far from complimentary.

"An' *you* – I serpose – one of the young divvils 'e picks up from 'Evving knows where. Told yer yer'd git a tanner, I serpose? Well, yer'll git a tanner if yer be'aves ter *my* likin', an' yer'll git a box on the ears if yer don'. Oh, come on, do; don't stand there orl night. 'Ere's the hapron – buns is a penny each, an' sangwiches a penny each, and cups o' corfy a penny each. Git a move on."

He was actually installed behind the counter. He was actually covered from neck to foot in a white apron. His rapture knew no bounds. He served strong men with sandwiches and cups of coffee. He dropped their pennies into the wooden till. He gave change (generally wrong). He turned the handle of the fascinating urn. He could not resist the handle of the little urn. When there were no customers he turned the handle, to see the little brown stream gush out in little spurts on to the floor or on to the counter.

His feeling of importance as he handed over buns and received pennies was indescribable. He felt like a king – like a god. He had forgotten all about his family . . .

Then the stout lady presented him with a bowl of hot water, a dishcloth, and a towel, and told him to wash up. Wash up! He had never washed up before. He swished the water round the bowl with the dishcloth very fast one way, and then quickly changed and swished it round the other. It was fascinating. He lifted the dishcloth high out of the water and swirled the thin stream to and fro. He soaked his apron and swamped the floor.

Finally, his patroness, who had been indulging in a doze, awoke and fixed eyes of horror upon him.

"What yer think yer a-doing of?" she said indignantly. "Yer think yer at the seaside, don't yer? Yer think yer've got yer little bucket an' spade, don't yer? Wastin' of good water – spoilin' of a good hapron. Where did 'Erb find *yer*, I'd like ter know. Picked yer aht of a lunatic asylum, *I* should say . . . Oh, lumme, 'ere's toffs comin'. Sharp, now, be ready wiv the hurn an' try an' 'ave a *bit* of sense, an' heverythin' double price fer toffs, now – don't forget."

But William, with a sinking heart, had recognised the toffs. Looking wildly round he saw a large cap (presumably 'Erb's) on a lower shelf of the stall. He seized it, put it on, and dragged it over his eyes. The "toffs" approached – four of them. One of them, the elder lady, seemed upset.

"Have you seen," she said to the owner of the stall, "a little boy anywhere about – a little boy in an Eton suit?"

"No, mam," said the proprietress, "I hain't seen no one in a heton suit."

"He was going out to a party," went on Mrs Brown breathlessly, "and he must have got lost on the way. They rang up to say he hadn't arrived, and the police have had no news of him, and we've traced him to this locality. You – you haven't seen a little boy that looked as if he were going to a party?"

"No, mam," said the lady of the coffee-stall. "I hain't seen no little boy goin' to no party this hevening."

"Oh, mother," said Ethel; and William, trying to hide his face between his cap brim and his apron, groaned in spirit as he heard her voice. "Do let's have some coffee now we're here."

"Very well, darling," said Mrs Brown. "Four cups of coffee, please."

William, still cowering under his cap, poured them out and handed them over the counter.

"You couldn't mistake him," said Mrs Brown tearfully. "He had a nice blue overcoat over his Eton suit, and a blue cap to match, and patent leather shoes, and he was *so* looking forward to the party, I can't think—"

"How much?" said William's father to William.

"Twopence each," muttered William.

There was a horrible silence.

"I beg your pardon," said William's father suavely, and William's heart sank.

"Twopence each," he muttered again.

There was another horrible silence.

"May I trouble you," went on William's father – and from the deadly politeness of his tone, William realised that all was over – "may I trouble you to remove your cap a moment? Something about your voice and the lower portion of your face reminds me of a near relative of mine—"

But it was Robert who snatched 'Erb's cap from his head and stripped his apron from him, and said: "You young devil!" and Ethel who said: "Goodness, just *look* at his clothes", and Mrs Brown who said: "Oh, my darling little William, and I thought I'd lost you"; and the lady of the coffee-stall who said: "Well, yer can *'ave* 'im fer all 'e knows abaht washin' up."

And William returned sad but unrepentant to the bosom of outraged Respectability.